Happy New Year!

I hope 2007 is going to be a great New Year for you. It certainly is going to be an exciting year for Harlequin Romance! We'll be bringing you:

More of what you love!

From February, six Harlequin Romances will be hitting the shelves every month. You'll find stories from your favorite authors, as well as some exciting new names, too!

A new date for your diary...

From February, you will find your Harlequin Romance books on sale from the **middle of the month.** (Instead of the beginning of the month.)

Most important, Harlequin Romance will continue to offer the kinds of stories you love—and more! From royalty to ranchers, bumps to babies, big cities to exotic desert kingdoms, these are emotional and uplifting stories, from the heart, for the heart!

So make a date with Harlequin Romance— in the middle of each month—and we promise it will be the most romantic date you'll make!

Happy reading!

Kimberley Young
Senior Editor

Dear Reader,

Welcome to the first story in my OUTBACK MARRIAGES duet. I could never have enough space to tell you how much I love my country, but my loyal readers will know I've been writing about it for the past thirty years. My aim at the beginning of my career was the same as now: to open a window on Australia for the pleasure, interest and expanding knowledge of our global readership. The first custodians of this vast land, the Australian Aborigines, have lived here for some sixty thousand years, and their presence has had an enormous bearing on the incredible mystique of the Outback. While the majority of the Australian population—a scant twenty million people, who live in a vastness of some three million square miles—cling to the lush corridor of coastlines, we're all very much aware of the great beating heart that lies beyond the rugged dividing ranges.

The focus of our national spirit belongs to the Man of the Outback. The Outback represents the real Australia. So much of my inspiration has been the heroic men and women that people the inland. Our cattle kings, our sheep barons and the men who work for them: heroes who, because of the extreme isolation of their workplace and the resulting lack of opportunities to meet partners, have had to devise some pretty bold strategies to find the right women with whom to share their lives and bear their children—young women ready and able to accept all the challenges that living in the Back O' Beyond brings.

My two heroes, Clay and Rory, recognize the indisputable fact that behind every good man stands an even better woman! See how Clay and Rory go about making two feisty heroines their own!

Good reading and warmest best wishes,

Margaret Way

MARGARET WAY
Outback Man Seeks Wife

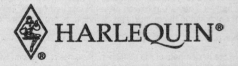

TORONTO • NEW YORK • LONDON
AMSTERDAM • PARIS • SYDNEY • HAMBURG
STOCKHOLM • ATHENS • TOKYO • MILAN • MADRID
PRAGUE • WARSAW • BUDAPEST • AUCKLAND

ISBN-13: 978-0-373-03927-2
ISBN-10:   0-373-03927-1

OUTBACK MAN SEEKS WIFE

First North American Publication 2007.

Copyright © 2006 by Margaret Way, Pty., Ltd.

Margaret Way takes great pleasure in her work and works hard at her pleasure. She enjoys tearing off to the beach with her family at weekends, loves haunting galleries and auctions, and is completely given over to French champagne "for every possible joyous occasion." She was born and educated in the river city of Brisbane, Australia, and now lives within sight and sound of beautiful Moreton Bay.

Margaret's anecdotes:

1. Outback people, like all people on the land, work extremely hard. They play hard, too. One only has to attend a gala Bachelor and Spinster Ball, or the legendary Birdsville Race Day—Birdsville is about as remote as it can get—to know that. Everyone enters wholeheartedly into the spirit of fun. Australians are great horse lovers. Not surprisingly, polo is the great game of the Outback and incredibly well attended. Whenever the opportunity arises to have fun and meet up with other Outback people, it's seized with both hands.

2. Outback people know how to have fun. Along with polo, rodeo events are popular, as well. The Alice rodeo in Alice Springs—the town at the very center of Australia—offers big prize money. Then there's the Camel Festival, and the hilarious Henley-on-Todd Regatta, where teams race in bottomless boats, leg-propelled down the dry, sandy bed of the river!

OUTBACK MARRIAGES
These bush bachelors are looking for a bride!

Welcome to Jimboorie—a friendly Outback town that sits among the striking red rocky landscape in the heart of Australia. This is where two rugged ranchers begin their quest for marriage.

Meet Clay Cunningham and Rory Compton—they're each searching for a wife, but will they find the right woman with whom to spend the rest of their lives?

Find out in this new duet from Margaret Way!

**This month, read all about Clay in
OUTBACK MAN SEEKS WIFE**

**And look out for Rory's story in March
CATTLE RANCHER, CONVENIENT WIFE**

CHAPTER ONE

'YOU CAN'T MISS HIM,' said a languid female voice from behind her. 'He's with the other guys making their way to the starting line. Dark blue shirt, yellow Number 6 on his back.'

Carrie McNevin turned her blond head. 'Your cousin, right?'

'Well *second* cousin!'

Carrie felt rather than saw the look of arrogant dismissal on Natasha Cunningham's face. 'I've barely spoken to him since he arrived.'

'Well you've made contact at least,' Carrie felt very sorry for the young man who had been treated so badly by his family. She couldn't remember Natasha's cousin herself. Or she *thought* she couldn't. There was some tiny spark of memory there. But she'd been little more than a toddler when he and his parents had disappeared from their part of the world like a puff of smoke.

'It was purely by accident I assure you,' Natasha retorted, with familiar derision.

There was a moment's respite from this edgy conversation while both young women followed the progress of the entries in the Jimboorie Cup, the main event in Jimboorie's annual two-day bush picnic races. The amateur jockeys, all fine horsemen, expertly brought their mounts under control. The horses, groomed to perfection, looked wonderful Carrie thought, the familiar excitement surging through her veins. She loved these special days when the closely knit but far flung Outback community came together from distances of hundreds of miles to relax and enjoy themselves. Many winged their way aboard their private planes. Others came overland in trucks, buses or their big dusty 4WD's sporting the ubiquitous bull bars. Outsiders joined in as well. City slickers out for the legendary good time to be had in the bush, inveterate race goers and gamblers who came from all over the country to mostly lose their money and salesmen of all kinds mixing with vast-spread station owners and graziers.

Picnic race days were a gloriously unique part of Outback Australia. The Jimboorie races weren't as famous as the Alice Springs or the Birdsville races with the towering blood-red sandhills of the Simpson Desert sitting just outside of town. Jimboorie lay further to the north-east, more towards the plains country at the centre of the giant state of Queensland with the surrounding stations running sheep, cattle or both.

It was early spring or what passed for spring; September so as to take advantage of the best weather of the year. Today's temperature was 27 degrees C. It was brilliantly fine—no humidity to speak of—but hotter around the bush course, which was located a couple of miles outside the small township of Jimboorie. It boasted *three* pubs—what could be sadder than an Outback town with no pub, worse no beer—all full up with visiting guests; a one man police station; a couple of government buildings; a small bush hospital manned by a doctor and two well qualified nurses; a chemist who sold all sorts of things outside of pharmaceuticals; a single room school; a post office that fitted neatly into a corner of the craft shop; a couple of shoe and clothing stores; a huge barn that sold just about everything like a city hyper-dome; the office of the well respected Jimboorie *Bulletin,* which appeared monthly and had a wide circulation. The branch office of the Commonwealth Bank had long since been closed down to everyone's disgust, but the town continued to boast a remarkably good Chinese restaurant and a bakehouse famous for the quality of its bread and its mouthwatering steak pies.

This afternoon the entire township of less than three thousand—a near boom town in the Outback—was in attendance, including the latest inhabitants, the publicans, Vince and Katie Dougherty's six-month-old identical twins, duly cooed over.

The horses, all with thoroughbred blood, were the pride of the competing stations; proud heads bowed, glossy necks arched, tails swishing in nervous anticipation. This was a special day for them, too. They were giving every indication they were ready to race their hearts out. All in all, though it was hidden beneath lots of laughter, back-slapping and the deeply entrenched mateship of the bush, rivalry was as keen as English mustard.

The Jimboorie Cup had been sponsored in the early days of settlement by the pioneering Cunningham family, a pastoral dynasty whose origins, like most others in colonial Australia, lay in the British Isles. William Cunningham second son of an English upper middle class rural family arrived in Australia in the early 1800s, going on to make his fortune in the southern colonies rearing and selling thousands of 'pure' Merino sheep. It wasn't until the mid-1860s that a branch of the family moved from New South Wales into Queensland, squatting on a few hundred thousand acres of rich black plains country, gradually moving from tin shed to wooden shack then into the Outback castles they eventually began to erect for themselves as befitting their social stature and to remind them of 'Home'.

Carrie's own ancestors—Anglo-Irish—had arrived ten years later in the 1870s with sufficient money to take up a huge run and eventually build a fine house some twenty miles distance from Jimboorie House the reigning queen. In time the Cunninghams and the McNevins and the ones who came after became known as the 'sheep barons' making great fortunes off the backs

of the Merinos. That was the boom time. It was wonderful while
it lasted and it lasted for well over one hundred years. But as
everyone knows for every boom there's a bust. The demand for
Australian wool—the best in the world—gradually went into
decline as man-made fibres emerged as strong competitors. The
smart producers had swiftly switched to sheep meat production
to keep afloat while still maintaining the country's fine wool
genetics from the dual purpose Merino. So Australia was still
riding on the sheep's back establishing itself as the world's
premium exporter of lamb.

The once splendid Jimboorie Station with its reputation for
producing the finest wool, under the guardianship of the incredibly stubborn and short-sighted Angus Cunningham had continued to focus on a rapidly declining market while his neighbours
had the good sense to turn quickly to diversification and sheep
meat production thus optimising returns.

Today the Cup was run by a *group* of station owners, working
extremely hard but still living the good life. Carrie's father, Bruce
McNevin, Clerk of the Course, was one. Natasha Cunningham's father another. Brad Harper, a relative newcomer—twenty
years—but a prominent station owner all the same, was the race
commentator and had been for a number of years. One of the horses—it was Number 6—Lightning Boy was acting extra frisky,
loping in circles, dancing on its black hooves, requiring its rider to
keep a good grip on the reins.

'He's an absolute nothing, a nobody,' Natasha Cunningham
continued the contemptuous tirade against her cousin. She came
alongside Carrie as she moved nearer the white rails. Flemington—
home of the Melbourne Cup—had its famous borders of beautiful
roses. Jimboorie's rails were hedged by thick banks of indestructible agapanthus waving their sunbursts of blue and white flowers.

'He certainly knows how to handle a horse,' Carrie murmured dryly.

'Why not? That's all he's ever been, a stockman. His father might have been one of us but his mother was just a common little slut. His father died early, probably from sheer boredom. He and his mother roamed Queensland towns like a couple of deadbeats, I believe. I doubt he's had much of an education. Mother's dead, too. Drink, drugs, probably both. The family never spoke one word to her. No one attended their wedding. Shotgun, Mother said.'

She *would,* Carrie thought, a clear picture of the acid tongued Julia Cunningham in her mind. Carrie thoroughly disliked the pretentious Julia and her even more snobbish daughter. Now she knew a moment of satisfaction. 'Well, your great uncle, Angus, remembered your cousin at the end. He left him Jimboorie.'

Natasha burst into bitter laughter. 'And what a prize that is! The homestead is just about ready to implode.'

'I've always loved it,' Carrie said with more than a touch of nostalgia. 'When I was little I thought it was a palace.'

'How stupid can you get!' Natasha gave a bark of laughter. 'Though I agree it would have been wonderful in the old days when the Cunninghams were the leading pioneering family. So of course we're still important. *My* grandfather would have seen to Jimboorie's upkeep. He would have switched to feeding the domestic market like Dad. But that old fool Angus never did a thing about it. Just left the station and the Cunningham ancestral home fall down around his ears. Went to pieces after his wife died and his daughter married and moved away. Angus should never have inherited in the first place. Neither should James. Or Clay as he calls himself these days. No 'little Jimmy' anymore. James Claybourne Cunningham. Claybourne, would you believe, was his mother's maiden name. A bit fancy for the likes of her.'

'It's a nice tribute to his mother,' Carrie said quietly. 'He can't have any fond memories of your side of the family.' What an understatement!

'Nor we for him! But the feud was on long before that. My grandad and great-uncle Angus hated one another. The whole Outback knows that.'

'Yes, indeed,' Carrie said, long acquainted with the tortured saga of the Cunninghams. She angled her wide brimmed cream hat so that it came further down over her eyes. The sun was blazing at three o'clock in the afternoon. A shimmering heat haze hovered over the track. 'Look, they're about to start.'

'Oh goody!' Natasha mocked the excitement in Carrie's voice. 'My money's on Scott.' She glanced sideways, her blue eyes filled with overt malice.

'So's mine,' Carrie answered calmly, visibly moving Scott's two carat diamond solitaire around on her finger. Natasha had always had her eye on Scott. It was in the nature of things Natasha Cunningham would always get what she wanted. But Scott had fallen for Carrie, very much upsetting the Cunninghams, and marking Carrie as a target for Natasha's vicious tongue. Something that had to be lived with.

Three races had already been run that afternoon. The crowd was in fine form calling for the day's big event to begin. There was a bit of larrikinism quickly clamped down on by Jimboorie's resident policeman. The huge white marquees acting as 'bars' had been doing a roaring trade. Scott, on the strapping Sassafras, a rich red chestnut with a white blaze and white socks, was the bookies' favourite, as well as the crowd's. He was up against two fine riders, members of his own polo team. No one had had any prior knowledge of the riding skills of the latest arrival to their far flung bush community. Well they knew *now,* Carrie thought. They only had to watch the way he handled his handsome horse. It had an excellent conformation; a generous chest that would have good heart room. The crowd knew who the rider was of course. Everyone knew his sad history. And there was *more!* All the girls for hundreds of miles around were agog with excitement having heard the rumour, which naturally spread like a bushfire, Clay Cunningham, a bachelor, was looking for a wife. That rivetting piece of information had come from Jimboorie's leading publican, the one and only Vince Dougherty. Vince gained it, he claimed, over a cold beer or two. Not that Clay Cunningham was the only bush bachelor looking for a wife. In the harsh and lonely conditions of the Outback—very much a man's world—eligible women were a fairly scarce commodity and thus highly prized. As far as Carrie could see all the pretty girls had swarmed here, some already joking about making the newcomer a good wife. Perhaps Clay Cunningham had been unwise to mention it. There was a good chance he'd get mobbed as proceedings got more boisterous.

He certainly cut a fine figure on horseback though Carrie didn't expect Natasha to concede that. The black gelding looked in tip-top condition. It had drawn almost as many admiring eyes as its rider. A fine rider herself—Carrie had won many ladies' races and cross country events—she loved to see good horsemanship. She hadn't competed in the Ladies' Race run earlier that day, which she most likely would have won. She was to present the Jimboorie Cup to the winning rider. Her mother, Alicia, President of the Ladies Committee and a woman of powerful persuasion, had insisted she look as fresh as a daisy and as glamorous as possible. A journalist and a photographer from a popular women's magazine had been invited to cover the two-day event with a gala dance to be held that night in Jimboorie's splendid new Community Hall of which they were all very proud.

A few minutes before 3:00 p.m. the chattering, laughing crowd abruptly hushed. They were waiting now for the starter, mounted on a distinguished old grey mare everyone knew as Daisy, to drop his white flag…Carrie began to count the seconds….

'They're off!' she shouted in her excitement, making a spontaneous little spring off the ground. A great cheer rose all around

her, lofting into the cloudless cobalt sky. The field, ten runners
in all, literally leapt from their standing start. The horses as was
usual were bunched up at first. Then the riders began battling for
good positions, two quickly becoming trapped on the rails. The
field sorted itself out and the horses began to pound along, hooves
eating up a track that was predictably hard and fast.

When the time came for the riders to negotiate the turn in
what was essentially a wild bush track, half of the field started
to fall back. In many ways it was more like a Wild West gallop
than the kind of sophisticated flat race one would see at a city
track. The front runners had begun to fight it out, showing their
true grit. Scott, his polo team mates and Jack Butler, who was
Carrie's father's overseer on Victory Downs. Clay Cunningham's black gelding was less than a length behind Jack and
going well. Carrie watched him lean forward to hiss some in-
struction into his horse's ear.

'Oh dear!' Carrie watched with a perverse mix of dismay and
delight as the gelding stormed up alongside Jack's gutsy
chestnut, then overtook him. Jack, who would have been thrilled
to be among the frontliners, was battling away for all he was
worth. At this rate Clay Cunningham was a sure thing, Carrie
considered, unless Scott could get some extra speed from his
mount. Scott was savagely competitive but the newcomer was
giving every indication he'd be hard to beat. One thing was
certain. Clay Cunningham was a crack rider.

Natasha, too, had drawn in her breath sharply. The possibility Scott could be beaten hadn't occurred to either woman.
Golden Boy Harper, as he was popularly known, was captain of
their winning polo team and thus had a special place in Jimboorie society.

'Your cousin looks like winning,' Carrie warned her, shaking
her own head. 'Damn it, *now,* Scott! Make your move.' Carrie
wasn't sure Scott was riding the right race. Though she would

never say it, she didn't actually consider Scott had the innate ability to get the best out of a horse. He didn't know much about *coaxing* for one thing.

Natasha belted the air furiously with her fist. 'This shouldn't be happening.'

'Well it *is!*' Carrie was preparing herself for the worst.

She saw Scott produce his whip, giving his horse a sharp crack, but Clay Cunningham was using touch and judgment rather than resorting to force. It paid off. The big black gelding had already closed the gap coming at full stride down the track.

'Damn it!' Natasha shrieked, looking ready to burst with disappointment.

Carrie, on the other hand, was feeling almost guilty. She was getting goose bumps just watching Clay Cunningham ride with such authority that Scott's efforts nearly fell into insignificance. That feeling in itself was difficult to come to grips with. The fast paced highly competitive gelding, like its rider, looked like it had plenty left in reserve.

Carrie held her breath, still feeling that upsurge of contrasting emotions. Admiration and apprehension were there aplenty. Sharp disappointment that Scott, her fiancé, wasn't going to win. Elation at how fast the big gelding was travelling—that was the horse lover in her she told herself. That animal had a lot of class. So did its rider. There was a man *determined* to win. After the way Jimboorie had treated him, Carrie couldn't begrudge him the victory. She liked a fighter.

Two minutes more, just as she expected, Lightning Boy flew past the post with almost two full lengths in hand.

What a buzz!

'Oh, well done!' Carrie cried, putting her hands together. For a moment she forgot she was standing beside Natasha, the inveterate informer. 'I wonder if he plays polo?' What an asset he would be!

'Of course he doesn't play polo,' Natasha snapped. 'He's a

pauper. Paupers don't get to play polo. Where's your loyalty anyway?' she demanded fiercely. 'Scott's your fiancé and you're applauding an outsider.'

'*Insider*,' Carrie corrected, looking as cool as a cucumber. 'He's already moved into Jimboorie.'

'For now.' Natasha made no effort to hide her outrage and anger. 'Just see if people deal with him. My father has a great amount of influence.'

Carrie frowned. 'What are you saying? Your family is readying to make life even more difficult for him?'

'You bet we are!' Natasha's blue eyes were hard. 'He'd be mad to stay around here. Old Angus only left him Jimboorie to spite us.'

'Be that as it may, your cousin must intend to stick around if he's looking for a wife,' Carrie said, really pleased that after a moment of stunned silence the crowd erupted into loud, appreciative applause and even louder whistles. They were willing to give the newcomer a fair go even if Natasha's vengeful family weren't. 'Well there you are!' she said brightly. 'No one rated his chances yet your cousin came out the clear winner.'

'We'll see what Scott has to say,' Natasha snorted with indignation, visibly jangling with nerves. 'For all we know there could have been interference near the fence.'

'There wasn't.' Carrie dismissed that charge very firmly. 'I know Scotty doesn't like to lose, but he'll take it well enough.' Some hope, she thought inwardly. Her fiancé had a considerable antipathy to losing. At anything.

'I'll be sure to tell him how delighted you were with my cousin's performance,' Natasha called quite nastily as she walked away.

'I bet you will,' Carrie muttered aloud. Since she and Scott had become engaged, two months previously, Natasha always gave Carrie the impression she'd like to tear her eyes out.

A tricky situation was now coming up. It was her job, graciously handed over to her by her mother, to present the Cup. Not to Scott, as just about everyone had confidently expected, but to the new owner of historic Jimboorie Station. The Cunningham ancestral home was falling down around his ears and the once premier cattle and sheep station these days was little more than a ruin said to be laden with debt. In all likelihood the new owner would at some stage sell up and move on. But for now, she had to find her way to the mounting yard for the presentation and lots of photographs. Come to that, she would have to take some herself. For two years now since she had returned home from university she had worked a couple of days a week for Paddy Kennedy, the founder and long time editor of the *Jimboorie Bulletin*. Once a senior editor with the *Sydney Morning Herald*, chronic life-threatening asthma sent him out to the pure dry air of the Outback where it was thought he had a better chance of controlling his condition.

That was twenty years ago. The monthly *Jimboorie Bulletin* wasn't any old rag featuring local gossip and kitty-up-the-tree stories. It was a professional newspaper, covering issues important to the Outback: the fragile environment, political matters, social matters, health matters, aboriginal matters, national sporting news, leavened by a page reporting on social events from all over the Outback. The rest of the time Carrie was kept busy with her various duties on the family station she loved, as well as running the home office, a job she had taken over from her mother.

Her work for the *Bulletin* stimulated her intellectually and she loved Paddy. He was the wisest, kindest man she knew whereas her father—although he had always been good to her in a material fashion—was not a man a *daughter* could get close to. A son maybe, but her parents had not been blessed with a son. She was an only child, one who was sensitive enough to have long become aware of her father's pain and bitter disappointment he had no male heir. He had already told her, although she would be well provided for, Victory Downs was to go to her cousin, Alex, the son of her father's younger brother. Uncle Andrew wasn't a pastoralist at all, though he had been raised in a pastoral family. He had a thriving law practice in Melbourne and was, in fact, the family solicitor.

Alex was still at university, uncertain what he wanted to be, although he knew Victory Downs would pass to him. Carrie's mother had fought aggressively for her daughter's rights but her father couldn't be moved. For once in her married life her mother had lost the fight.

'You know how men are!' Alicia had railed. 'They think women can't run anything. It's immensely unfair. How can your father think young Alex would be a better manager than you?'

'That's not the only reason, Mum,' Carrie had replied, thinking it terrible to be robbed of one's inheritance. 'Dad doesn't want the station to pass out of the family. Sons have to be the inheritors. Sons carry the family name. Dad doesn't care at all for the idea anyone other than a McNevin should inherit Victory Downs. He seems to be naturally suspicious of women as well. Why is that? Uncle Andy isn't a bit like that.'

'Your father just doesn't know how to relax,' was Alicia's stock explanation, always turning swiftly to another topic.

It had been strange growing up knowing she was seriously undervalued by her father but Carrie was reluctant to criticise him. He was a *good* father in his way. Certainly she and her mother lacked for nothing, though there was no question of squandering money like Julia Cunningham, who spent as much time in the big cities of Sydney and Melbourne as she did in her Outback home.

People in the swirling crowd waved to her happily—she waved back. Most of the young women her age were wearing smart casual dress, while she was decked out as if she were attending a garden party at Government House in Sydney. Alicia's idea. Carrie's hat was lovely really, the wide dipping brim trimmed with silk flowers. She wore a sunshine-yellow printed silk dress sent to her from her mother's favourite Sydney designer. Studded high heeled yellow sandals were on her feet. Her long honey-blond hair was drawn back into a sophisticated knot to accommodate the picture hat her mother had insisted on her wearing.

'I want you to look really, *really* good!' Alicia, a classic beauty in her mid-forties and looking nothing like it, fussed over her. 'Which means you have to wear this hat. It will protect your lovely skin for one thing as well as adding the necessary glamour. Never forget it's doubly essential to look after one's skin in our part of the world. You know how careful I am even though we have an enviable tawny tint.'

Indeed they had. Carrie had inherited her mother's beautiful brown eyes as well. Eyes that presented such a striking contrast to their golden hair. Carrie, christened Caroline Adriana McNevin had *no* look of her father's side of the family. She didn't really mind. Alicia, from a well-to-do Melbourne family and with an Italian Contessa as her maternal grandmother, was a beautiful woman by anyone's standards.

'You're a lucky girl, do you realise that? Scott Harper for a fiancé.' Alicia fondly pinched her daughter's cheek. 'I don't think the Cunninghams will ever get over it. Julia worked so hard to throw Scott and Natasha together.'

As if you didn't do the same thing with Scott and me, Mamma, Carrie thought but didn't have the heart to say. Scott Harper was one of the most eligible bachelors in the country. His father's property ventures were huge. Even Carrie's father had been 'absolutely delighted' when she and Scott had become engaged. Obviously the best thing a daughter could do—her crowning achievement as it were—was to marry a handsome young man from a wealthy family. To prove it her father seemed to have a lot more time for her in the past few months. Could he be thinking of future heirs, not withstanding the fact he had already made a will in favour of Alex? It wouldn't be so bad, would it, to pass Victory Downs on to someone like Scott Harper, rich and ambitious?

Sometimes Carrie felt like a pawn.

Clay was agreeably surprised by the number of people who made it their business to congratulate him. Many of the older generation mentioned they remembered his father and added how much Clay resembled him. One sweet-faced elderly lady actually asked after his mother, her smile crumpling when Clay told her gently that his mother had passed on. He hadn't received any congratulations from the runner-up, the god in their midst, Scott Harper, and didn't expect any. Leopards didn't change their spots. Aged ten when his parents uprooted him from the place he so loved and which incredibly was now his, Clay still had vivid memories of Scott Harper, the golden-haired bully boy, two years his senior. Harper had treated him like trash when he'd never had trouble from the other station boys. For some reason Harper had baited him mercilessly about his parents' marriage whenever they met up. Once Harper had knocked him down in the main street of the town causing a bad concussion for which he'd been hospitalised. His father, wild as hell, had made the long drive in his battered utility to the Harper station to remonstrate with Scott's father, but he had been turned back at gunpoint by Bradley Harper's men.

Clay's taking the Jimboorie Cup from Scott this afternoon was doubly sweet. Soon the surprisingly impressive silver cup would be presented to him by Harper's fiancé. He had been amazed to hear it was Caroline McNevin, whom he remembered as the prettiest little girl he had ever laid eyes on. How had that exquisite little creature grown up to become engaged to someone like Harper? But then wasn't it a tradition for pastoral families to intermarry? His father—once considered destined for great things—had proved the odd man out, struck down by love at first sight. Love for a penniless little Irish girl now buried by his side.

There was a stir in the crowd. Clay turned about to see a woman coming towards him. He drew himself up straighter, absolutely thrown by how beautiful Caroline had become. Her whole aura suggested springtime, a world of flowers. Her petite figure absorbed all the sunlight around her.

She seemed to *float* rather than walk. For a moment an overwhelming emotion swept over him. To combat it, he stood very, very still. He wondered if it were nostalgia; remembrance of some lovely moment when he was a boy. The hillsides around Jimboorie alight with golden wattle, perhaps?

Now they were face-to-face, less than a metre apart, and he like a fool stood transfixed. He was conscious his nerves had tensed and his stomach muscles had tightened into a hard knot. She was *tiny* compared to him. Even in her high heels she only came up to his heart. She still had that look of shining innocence, only now it was allied to an adult allure all the more potent since both qualities appeared to exist quite naturally side by side.

He couldn't seem to take his eyes off her while she consolidated her hold over him.

Caroline had beautiful large oval eyes, a deep velvety-brown. They were doubly arresting with her golden hair. Her skin, a tawny olive beneath the big picture hat, was flawlessly beautiful. Her features were delicate, perfectly symmetrical. No more than five-three, she nevertheless had a real presence. At least she was running tight circles around him.

'James Cunningham!' The vision smiled at him. A smile that damn near broke his heart. What the heck was the matter with him? How could he describe what he felt? Perhaps they had meant something to each other in another life? 'Welcome back to Jimboorie. I'm Carrie McNevin.'

Belatedly he came back to control. 'I remember you, Caroline,' he said, his voice steady, unhurried, yet he was so broad-sided by her beauty, he forgot to smile.

'You *can't*!' A soft flush rose to her cheeks.

'I do.' He shrugged his shoulder, thinking beautiful women had unbounded power at their pink fingertips. 'I remember you as the happy little girl who used to wave to me when you saw me in town.'

'Really?' She was enchanted by the idea.

'Yes, really.'

Her essential sweetness enfolded him. Her voice was clear and gentle, beautifully enunciated. Caroline McNevin, the little princess. Untouchable. Except now by Harper. That made him hot and angry, inducing feelings that hit him with the force of a breaker.

'Well, it's my great pleasure, James, or do you prefer to be called Clay?' She paused, tipping her golden head to one side.

'Clay will do.' Only his mother had ever called him James. Now he remembered to smile though his expression remained serious even a little sombre. Why wouldn't he when he felt ap-pallingly vulnerable in the face of a beautiful creature who barely came up to his heart?

Carrie was aware of the sombreness in him. It added to the impression he gave of quiet power and it had to be admitted, mystery. 'Then it's going to be my great pleasure to be able to present you, Clay, with the Jimboorie Cup,' Carrie continued. 'We'll just move back over there,' she said, turning to lead the way to a small dais where the race committee was grouped, waiting for her and the winner of the Cup to join them. 'They'll want to take photos,' she told him, herself oddly shaken by their meeting. And the feeling wasn't passing off. Perhaps it was because she'd heard so many stories about the Cunninghams while she was growing up? Or maybe it was because Clay Cun-ningham had grown into a strikingly attractive man. She felt that attraction brush over her then without her being able to do a thing about it. She felt it sink into her skin. She only hoped she wasn't showing her strong reactions. Everyone was looking at them.

Natasha might well continue to denounce her cousin, Carrie thought, but the family resemblance was strong. The Cunninghams were a handsome lot, raven haired, with bright blue eyes. Natasha would have been beautiful, but her fine features were marred by inner discontent and her eyes were strangely cold. Clay Cunningham had the Cunningham height and rangy build—only his hair wasn't black. It was a rich mahogany with a flame of dark auburn as the sun burnished it. His eyes, the burning blue of an Outback sky, were really beautiful, full of depth and sparkle. He looked like a *real* man. A man women would fall for hook, line and sinker. So why wasn't he married already, or actively looking for a wife? If indeed the rumour were true. Something she was beginning to doubt. He had to be four, maybe five years older than she, which made him around twenty-eight. He was a different kind of man from Scott. She sensed a depth, a sensitivity—whatever it was—in him that Scott lacked.

It had to be an effect of the light but there seemed to be sparkles in the space between them. Carrie never dreamed a near-stranger could have this effect on her. Her main concern was to conceal it. Up until now she had felt *safe*. She was going to marry Scott, the man she was in love with—yet Clay Cunningham's blue gaze had reached forbidden places.

Their hands touched as she handed over the Silver Cup to the accompanying waves of applause. She couldn't move, even *think* for a few seconds. She felt a little jolt of electricity through every pore of her skin. He continued to hold her eyes, his own unfaltering. Had her trembling transferred itself to him like a vibration? She hoped not. She wasn't permitted to feel like this.

Yet sparkles continued to pulsate before her eyes. Perhaps she was mildly sun-struck? She had the unnerving notion that the little frisson of shock—unlike anything she had ever experi-

enced before—was mutual. She even wondered what life might
have in store if he decided to remain on Jimboorie? All around
her people were laughing and clapping. Some were carrying col-
ourful balloons. The thrill of the race had got to her. That was it!
Her course was set. She was a happily engaged woman. She was
to marry Scott Harper in December. A Christmas bride.

And there was Scott staring right at her. Too late she became
aware of him. She felt the chill behind his smile. She knew him
so well she had no difficulty recognising it. It came towards her
like an ice-bearing cloud. He was furious and doing a wonderful job of hiding it. A triumphant looking Natasha was by his side,
the two of them striking a near identical pose; one full of an over-
bearing self-confidence. Maybe arrogance was a better word.
Scott as Bradley Harper's heir certainly liked to flaunt it.
Natasha, as a Cunningham, did too.

Now Scott sauntered towards the dais around which the VIPs
of the vast district milled, calling in a taunting voice, 'You'll absolutely have to tell us, *Jimmy,* where you learned how to ride
like that? And the name of the guy who loaned you his horse. Or
did you steal it?' He held up defensive hands. 'Only joking!'

As a joke it was way off, but Clay Cunningham held his
ground, quite unmoved. 'You haven't changed one little bit, have
you, Harper?' he said with unruffled calm. 'Lightning Boy was
a parting gift from a good friend of mine. A beauty, isn't he? He
could run the race over.'

'Like to give it another go?' Scott challenged with an open
lick of hostility.

'Any time—when *your* horse is less spent.' Clay Cunningham
gently waved the silver cup aloft to another roar of applause.

Bruce McNevin, a concerned observer to all this, fearing a
confrontation, moved quickly onto the dais to address the crowd.
Even youngsters draped over the railings managed to fall silent.
They were used to hearing from Mr. McNevin who was to say a

few words then hand over the prize money of $20,000 dollars, well above the reward offered by other bush committees.

Her father was a handsome man, Carrie thought proudly. A man in his prime. He had a full head of dark hair, good regular features, a bony Celtic nose, a strong clean jawline and well defined cheekbones. He was always immaculately if very conservatively dressed. Bruce McNevin was definitely a 'tweedy' man.

While her father spoke Carrie stood not altogether happily within the half circle of Scott's distinctly proprietorial arm. She was acutely aware of the anger and dented pride he was fighting to hold in. Scott wasn't a good loser. Carrie didn't know why but it was apparent he had taken an active dislike to Clay Cunningham.

Now Clay Cunningham, cheque in hand, made a response to her father that proved such a mix of modesty, confidence and dry humour that time and again his little speech was punctuated by appreciative bursts of laughter and applause. The crowd was still excited and the winner's speech couldn't have been more designed to please. The race goers had come to witness a good race and the Cup winner—a newcomer—had well and truly delivered. Not that anyone could really call him a newcomer. Heavens, he was a Cunningham! Cunningham was a name everyone knew. There was even a chance he might be able to save what was left of that once proud historic station, Jimboorie, though it would take a Herculean effort and a bottomless well of money.

'Who the hell does he think he is?' Scott muttered in Carrie's ear, unable to credit the man 'little Jimmy' Cunningham, the urchin, had become. 'And what's with the posh voice?'

'He *is* a Cunningham, Scott,' Carrie felt obliged to point out. 'It's written all over him. And it may very well be he *did* get a good education.'

Scott snorted like an angry bull. His father left here without a dime. Everyone knows that. Angus Cunningham might have sheltered them to spite the rest of his family but he couldn't have paid his nephew anything in the way of wages. Reece Cunningham cut himself off from his own family when he married that little tramp.'

'You know nothing about her, Scott.' Carrie pulled away from him as discreetly as she could. '*My* mother says there was *no* proof whatsoever to any of the cruel stories that were circulated about her by the Cunninghams and the Campbells. Remember Clay's father was expected to marry Elizabeth Campbell or Campbell-Moore as she is today.'

'But the fool of a man didn't,' Scott retorted, staring down at her with a mixture of hurt and displeasure. 'Whose side are you on anyway?'

She turned away from the glare in his eyes. 'The side of fair mindedness, Scott. Now you'll have to excuse me. Mamma wants me for more photographs.'

'Go to her by all means.' Scott bowed slightly. 'I just hope Cunningham doesn't plan on showing up tonight.'

His voice was iron hard.

CHAPTER TWO

WRESTLING with her unsettled feelings, Carrie dressed for the gala dance. Her party dress at least gave her uncomplicated pleasure. It was of white silk chiffon, feminine and floaty. White always married well with the golden tint in her skin, a legacy of that generous dollop of Italian blood. The bodice of her evening dress was perfectly plain, dipping low into the cleft between her breasts and hung from double spaghetti straps. The midcalf swishy skirt was richly embroidered with swirls of tiny seed pearls and silver sequins. She wore her hair hanging loose down her back—the way Scott liked it—but pulled away from her face and secured behind her ears with two beautiful antique hair combs encrusted with dazzling faux jewels. She should have felt on top of the world, instead she felt...*apprehensive* as though something unpleasant was going to happen or she was going to make a single irreversible mistake. So that's what meeting up with Clay Cunningham had done for her!

Her mind kept jumping back to the look in Scott's eyes. The hardness, the jealousy and the defiance. Scott scarcely knew Clay Cunningham. Scott could only have been twelve when Clay's father had finally packed up and moved his family away, but she could have sworn Scott's antagonism to Clay Cunningham, perhaps buried deep within him, had re-surfaced with a vengeance. She already knew about Scott's jealous nature, but usually he kept it under control. Scott actually disliked even his own friends smiling at her let alone attempting a playful flirtation. It was a terrifying thought he might have intuited her spontaneous reaction to the man Clay Cunningham had grown into. She realised, too, with a guilty pang ever since Clay had told her she used to wave to him in the town when she was a little girl, she had been trying very hard to evoke a forgotten memory.

Goodness, what's the matter with me? she asked her reflection. She was usually very level-headed. She even felt an impulse to start praying the evening would go well. Glancing up at the silver framed wall clock she saw it was almost eight. She really should be on her way. Scott was going to meet her in the foyer It was only a short walk from Dougherty's pub where she was staying to the new Community Hall. The band had been underway for at least an hour, the infectious toe tapping music spilling out onto the street. The band was good. Her mother had arranged for the musicians to come from Brisbane. She started to sing along a little, trying to lift her spirits.

A final check in the mirror. Turning her head from side to side, she saw the sparkling light of her hair combs, one of innumerable little presents from her mother. Her parents were staying overnight with friends. She had elected to stay with Vince and Katie at the pub, as they always looked after her. The pub was spotlessly clean, the food not fancy, but good. She stayed there overnight when she was working for Paddy at the *Bulletin*. It was preferable to making the long drive home, then back again the following morning. Victory Downs was over a hundred miles west of the town—no distance in the bush—but she had to multiply that by four when she worked in town as she mostly did, two days in a row.

She had her silver sandalled foot on the second bottom tread of the staircase when Scott, wearing a white dinner jacket, and looking dazzlingly handsome, swung through the front doors.

'Hiyah, beautiful!' His blue eyes travelled over her with pride of possession. 'I *am* impressed!'

The overhead light glinted on his smooth golden hair and the white of his smile. If they had children—she wanted three, four was okay—they were bound to have golden hair, Carrie thought, holding out her hands to him.

'There's not going to be anyone to touch you!' Scott continued to eye her, appreciatively. She looked as good to eat as a bowl of vanilla ice cream. He'd had a lot of girls over the years but Carrie was unique.

'You look great yourself!' she told him, sincerity in her velvety eyes.

'All for you.' He'd had a few drinks: now, he badly wanted pull her into his arms. He wanted to race her back upstairs, strip that pretty white dress off her, throw her down on the bed and make violent love to her. Only he was afraid of what might happen. Carrie, by his reckoning, had to be the last virgin over fifteen left on the planet. If that weren't astonishing enough, she wanted it to remain that way until they were married. Could you beat it! He would *never* have agreed, only he saw her resolve was very strong. Or maybe she was playing it smart, teasing the living daylights out of him. She was his fiancée yet he had to keep his hands off her. Well, within limits. It was excruciatingly frustrating—more torture—when she filled him with such lust as he had ever known. Not that he had taken a corresponding vow of celibacy. He got release when he wanted it. Most girls were his for the asking including that bitch Natasha Cunningham. He'd had an on and off relationship with her for years. She was mad for him—and he knew it.

But it was innocent little Caroline McNevin he had always wanted. He guessed he had started to want her from when she was a yummy little teenager with budding breasts. He'd confidently thought virginity was a relic of the Dark Ages. He'd been stunned when Carrie told him she wanted to remain a virgin until their wedding night. At first he'd been sure it was a damned ploy to keep him interested, on a knife's edge. As a ploy it certainly worked, but then he came to realise she was fair dinkum. It was impossible to believe! But, boy, wouldn't he make up for the long hungry years of deprivation! Their wedding night couldn't come soon enough.

They had scarcely made it into the packed hall with huge silver-blue disco balls suspended from the ceiling like glittering moons, when Scott's grip on her arm tightened. Carrie let out a surprised little whimper. 'Hey, Scott, you're hurting!'

'Sorry.' He shifted his arm to around her waist, hauling her close to him. 'That bastard has had the nerve to show up,' he ground out, his eyes quickly finding Clay Cunningham's rangy figure across the room.

So it wasn't going to be a happy evening! Carrie's heart began to thump. She lifted her eyes to Scott's tight face. 'Scott, please settle down. We're here to enjoy ourselves aren't we? Everybody will be watching. Clay Cunningham has a perfect right to be here. I expect there would be a lot of disappointed girls if he hadn't shown up. Surely you're not looking for trouble?'

'He'd do well to steer clear of me,' Scott gritted, unable to conceal a flare of jealousy so monstrous it startled even him. He tried to calm himself by sheer will power. So far as he was concerned it was Cunningham versus *him!* Across the packed hall Cunningham was standing head and shoulders above a group of silly giggling females. One let out a burst of ecstatic laughter, obviously thrilled there was an eligible bachelor in their midst. A man, moreover, who had expressed his desire to find himself a wife. Hadn't they heard, the little fools, Jimboorie House was falling down? Didn't they know Jimboorie Station would never be what it was again? Or would any man do? Girls fell in and out of love so fast. They were like kids with some wonderful new toy.

All right, Cunningham was handsome. Scott was honest enough to admit that. All the Cunninghams were. Even Natasha. And Cunningham had that look about him, he recognised, of a fine natural athlete. How had that little weed of a kid who he'd loved slapping around turned into this guy? Scott wasn't even sure he could take Cunningham in a fight, even though he was a good amateur boxer, a welterweight champion at university. The fact Cunningham had beaten him for the Cup Scott took as a scalding defeat. And he'd been beaten so *easily!* That was what stunned and humiliated him. He was used to being king pin. To cap it off his fiancée had presented Cunningham with the Cup. He'd watched their eyes, then their hands meet. It had only taken him a second to register the look on Carrie's face. It had filled him with jealousy and unease.

Cunningham had stirred her interest and attention. That wasn't going to be allowed to happen. Carrie was *his*! He owned her. Or near enough. She was wearing his ring.

I mightn't be able to stop you looking, but don't touch, you bastard! Scott swung Carrie into his arms, whisking her onto the dance floor. At least the music was great. It filled up the room.

After each bracket of numbers, the crowd clapped their appreciation. One of the band, a sexy looking guy in tight jeans, a red satin shirt and cowboy boots, took over the microphone to a roar of applause and began to sing, launching into the first romantic ballad of the night; one that was currently top of the charts. His voice was so attractive the dancers gave themselves up to it....

Carrie didn't have the usual succession of dance partners she'd had in the past. Things had changed since she had become engaged to Scott. She realised she was starting to worry that Scott was so possessive. She wasn't *property*. She was a woman, a human being. The last thing she wanted was a stormy married life with a control freak for a husband. But then her thoughts turned to how understanding Scott was about her desire to remain a virgin until their marriage. It pleased her that he was so considerate of her wishes. She had never been one to bow to peer pressure so she hadn't been part of the general sexual experimentation that had attended her university years. She knew some of her fellow students had labelled her a bit of an extremist, but the idea of sex without genuine strong feeling had little appeal for her. It was *her* body that would be invaded after all. Men came from a different place. Most of them she had found, saw sex as satisfying an appetite like food and drink. At the same time they were notoriously quick to pin cruel labels on their willing female partners. Carrie thought there was not only a moral standard, but a health standard that made fastidiousness matter.

Then again she had to take stock of the fact she had no real conflict with remaining a virgin. There was even the odd moment when she had to consider perhaps she hadn't met the man who could overturn all her defences? Or maybe her libido wasn't of the intense sort? Not that Scott hadn't awakened her romantic desires. He had. She knew about sensual pleasure. But still it had been relatively easy to keep to her vow. Or it had been up until now.

She was momentarily alone. Scott was caught up in settling an argument about some polo match when she heard her name— her *full* name—spoken.

'You dance beautifully, Caroline. Will you dance with me?'

He was standing in front of her, looking down at her from his superior height. The corners of his mouth were upturned in a smile. His dark blue eyes held a current of electricity that bathed her in its glow.

She managed to smile back. It felt like taking a risk. A tremble shook her body. The music…the laughter…the voices…oddly started to recede. She knew her lips parted but for the smallest time—maybe a few seconds—no words came out.

'Caroline?'

The oxygen came back to her brain. 'Yes of course I will,' she said, unaware a nerve was pulsing in the hollow of her throat.

His arms came around her. He held her lightly yet his arms enclosed her. Letting him hold her—she knew—vastly increased the risks.

She couldn't relax. Not there and then. He was, she realised, gifted with sexual radiance and he was using that gift. Consciously or unconsciously? She couldn't tell.

She tried to distract herself by looking at the sea of happy, excited faces around them.

'I know, I'm too tall for you.' Clay's voice was wry. 'And I'm not much of a dancer. Never had time to learn.'

'No, you're fine.' Indeed, it seemed to her he moved with natural ease and rhythm.

'And you're kind.' He pulled her in a little closer and she lifted her hand higher on his shoulder. She could feel the strength in it; the warmth of his skin. He wasn't formally attired like Scott . He wore a beige coloured linen jacket over a black T-shirt and black jeans. A simple outfit, yet on him it looked very sophisticated. He would have absolutely no difficulty finding a wife. In fact, the frenzy had already started. It was her role to watch. Never let it be forgotten she was taken!

She realised she was luxuriating in his clean male scent, redolent of the open air, of fragrant wood smoke. Inhaled, it left her with a feeling akin to a delicious languor. The overhead disco lights dazzled, throwing out blue and silver rays over the swirling crowd, their faces and clothes streaked with light.

For long minutes they danced without speaking, he leading her expertly for all he claimed he couldn't dance. She was beginning to feel a degree of trepidation at the forces set loose by their physical contact. She didn't want it. She certainly didn't need it. She didn't even understand it. Her reaction wasn't *normal*. She couldn't allow herself to think it was akin to being in a state of thrall!

Be careful with this! A warning voice said.

There was a pressure behind Carrie's rib cage. Could he incite emotion as easily as he could incite his high mettled horse to victory? She feared that might be the case. It was even possible he could be looking at *her* as a conquest? Retribution for the way he had been treated? A perverted desire to win over Scott Harper's fiancée? She saw how he had won the Cup. His was a powerful determination and maybe she was next on his list? Only time would prove her right.

Meanwhile he was making her feel decidedly odd. It was as if she were someone else. She couldn't allow that. She had to be herself, yet the feel of his arms around her had deep chords resounding within her. His hand on her back could even be playing her like a master musician. What was he really thinking?

'You look very beautiful,' he said. His voice, which was resonant and deep, had considerable emotional power.

Carrie took a quick breath, thinking she wasn't going to give him any help.

'Harper is a lucky man.'

Now she tilted her head to stare into his eyes. 'What went wrong between you two? It seems strange—you were both so young when you moved away, yet I sense a history between you and Scott. An animosity that still clings.'

The flash in his eyes was as blue as an acetate flame. 'Scott Harper used to like to scare me when I was a kid.'

She felt shame on Scott's behalf. 'It still matters?'

He shrugged. 'You saw how your fiancé was. I'm sure he'll be right with us any moment now. Do you mind that most of the guys here, though they're dying to dance with you, are keeping their distance?'

That hit home. 'I *do* realise,' she said, more severely than she had intended, 'but Scott is my fiancé.'

He nodded. 'A pity'

'A pity he's my fiancé?' Now she was really on the defensive.

'How do you know I don't want you for myself?' He unfolded a slow smile, keeping his tone light.

Hectic colour swept into her cheeks, enhancing her beauty. 'I'm sorry, Clay, but I'm taken.'

'Have you set a date for the wedding?' he asked, with interest.

'Why aren't *you* married?' she countered, aware something potentially dangerous was smouldering between them.

'Because I believe a man has to be able to provide for a wife before he embarks on matrimony.'

She realised she was becoming agitated. She had to rein herself in. 'The rumour around town is you're looking for a wife. Could that possibly be right?'

His smile was self mocking. 'You might very well see me on the doorstep of the *Bulletin* some time soon. I understand you're Pat Kennedy's right hand woman. You can help me run an ad. "Bush Bachelor Seeks A Wife!" You could advise me what to say, maybe help me read through what replies come in.'

'You're joking!' She felt an odd anger.

Clay's blue, blue eyes were alight with what? Devilment? A taunt? He was still holding her lightly but she was starting to feel she couldn't breathe.

'I couldn't be more serious,' he replied. 'I want a wife beside me. I want children. I've been so flat-out working all my life, I've had little time to play the courting game. Besides, eligible young women aren't all that easy to find. I thought an ad might work. It would certainly speed things up.'

He was obviously waiting for her response.

It came out soft but tart. 'Why don't you simply walk up to one of the girls here?' Carrie challenged him, wishing she was older, taller, more experienced. As it was she was a little afraid of him.

He wasn't smiling. 'Forgive me, but it's hard to see past you.'

That transfixed her. She, so light on her feet, a lovely dancer, missed a step, nearly causing him to tread on her toe. 'Must I remind you that I'm taken?' she said as though he had broken a strict rule.

'So you are!' His voice was deeply regretful.

What should she do? Walk away? Abandon him on the dance floor? She didn't *want* to. At the same time she knew she had to.

Run, run away! Far from temptation!

'Give yourself plenty of time to make sure it's going to work.' He steered her away from a whirling couple.

'Is that a warning?' This man was deliberately casting a spell on her. To what end?

'I don't see the two of you together,' he said.

'How can you possibly judge?' Despite herself she began to compare him with Scott. It was something she couldn't control. 'You don't know me and you don't know Scott. We have a fine future ahead of us.'

'Why, then, the fright in your eyes? If he's the love of your life?'

There was such a whirring inside her. It was as though some part of her hitherto not properly in working order, suddenly sprang into life. 'Why are we talking like this, Clay? It's getting very personal and private.' Not to say out of order.

'I told you. I don't have much time. Besides, I feel I could talk to you far into the night.'

'You've just told me why.' She pointed out, not without sarcasm. 'You're lonely.'

'It's possible that's part of it,' he agreed smoothly.

Carrie sucked in her breath; waited a moment. 'I must tell you I wouldn't have agreed to marry Scott if I didn't love him.' Now her voice sounded stilted.

'As I said, Harper is a very lucky man.'

This was too much. Just *too* much. She couldn't play this game if that's what it was. Dancing with him wasn't the same as dancing with Scott. Or any other man for that matter. She could feel the blood beating in her throat, in her breasts, in the pit of her stomach. She had never been so breathtakingly conscious of her own *flesh*.

The same tipsy couple almost careened into them. Clay's arm tightened around her as he swiftly drew her out of harm's way.

She knew it was well past the time to break away, but she made the excuse to herself that would only draw attention to them. So change the subject quickly! 'You're not planning to leave, then?'

'Caroline, I've just arrived,' he replied, mock-plaintively.

'Everyone calls me Carrie.' She spoke as if to correct him when in reality the sound of her name on his lips was like a bell tolling inside her.

'I'm not everyone,' he said quietly. 'Carrie is pretty. Caroline suits you better.'

'What if I say I want you to call me Carrie?'

'All right, Carrie.' He smiled. 'I'll call you Caroline whenever I get the chance.'

It was totally unnerving how dramatically he was getting to her. 'I used to think when I was little that Jimboorie House was a palace.'

'So did I.' Again his glance like blue flame rested on her.

'You have more than a trace of an English accent. Where did that come from?'

He looked over her blond head. 'From my mother I guess. She was Anglo-Irish and well spoken—and lovely. My father's appallingly cruel family had no right to treat her the way they did. They turned all their fury on *her* because my father abandoned them for her. The accent would have been reinforced by long contact with my late mentor who was English. I became very close to him.'

'Was he the one who presented you with Lightning Boy?' She wanted to know all about him.

He nodded. 'Yes, he was. He handed Lightning Boy over a couple of months before he died.'

She read the grief in his glance. 'What did you do? Did you work for him?'

'I was proud to,' he said briefly, his tone a little curt. 'My boss and mentor.'

'Are you going to tell me his name?'

'No, Caroline.' He refused her. At the same time his gaze gathered her up.

'I'm sorry.' She glanced across the dance floor at all the glowing, happy faces. This would go on into the wee hours. 'I won't intrude. I'm just glad you met someone who treated you well.'

'I can't recall many others.' His expression was openly bitter.

'Are you going to make us all pay for wounding you?' she asked, thinking he had been hurt a great deal.

He ignored her question. 'I'd like to take you out to Jimboorie. Would you come?'

Her heart jumped. Agree and there'd be trouble. *Big* trouble.

'Look at me,' he invited quietly. 'Not away. Would you come, Caroline?'

A back-up singer in the band launched into a romantic number. 'How do you see me?' she countered. 'As someone whose freedom is being curtailed?'

'Is it?' He studied her so intently he might have been trying to unmask her.

That put her on her mettle. 'I'd be delighted to come,' she said shortly, consoling herself she had been driven to it.

'Good. I confess I find a woman's views necessary.'

'Is it your intention to put in your ad that Jimboorie House is falling down?' She met his eyes.

'Certainly. It's the right thing to do,' he replied smoothly.

'But it's not in the utter state of decay it appears to be from the outside. The best materials were used in its construction. The finest, stoutest timbers. The cedar came from the vast forests of the Bunya Bunya Mountains. The house itself is built of sandstone. There *is* a tremendous amount of restoration to be done—I can't deny that—but somehow I'll get around it.'

'Perhaps you should say in your ad that you're looking for an heiress?' she suggested, bitter-sweet.

'Now that's a great idea.' His face broke into a mocking smile.

Unnoticed by either of them Scott Harper, who had been further detained by two of his father's friends wanting to know if he thought his team could continue their unbeaten polo season, was quickly canvassing the crowd.

The blood flooded into his face the moment he saw them together. He drew in his breath sharply, catching his bottom lip between strong teeth and drawing blood. How could Carrie possibly do this thing? She knew how he felt about Clay Cunningham. All his childhood antipathy had returned but one hundred times worse. He made his way towards them, threading a path through the dancers, some of them, marking his expression, getting out of his way.

Just look at her, Scott inwardly raged, his jealousy violent and painful. Her beautiful blond head was tipped right back as she stared up into Cunningham's eyes.

This is wrong, all wrong. Let her go!

His progress was stopped when a woman got him in a surprisingly strong arm-lock. 'Scotty, you're not ignoring me are you, darling?'

He swung, catching the hateful expression of malice on Natasha's face. 'You can't let your dewy little fiancée have a bit of fun, can you?' Her voice dropped so low he could barely hear her. 'And she *is* having fun, isn't she?'

'Let go, Natasha,' he rasped. If she'd been a man he would have hit her, so tense was his mood.

'Sure. One dance and we'll call it a night.' She stepped right up to him, a stunning figure in violet banded in silver, putting both hands on his shoulders. 'Don't make a fool of me now, Scotty,' she warned. 'I've kept my mouth shut up to now, but things can change.'

'You're a real bitch! You know that?' he muttered, contempt built into his voice. Nevertheless he retained enough sense to draw her into his arms.

'You don't say that when I'm making you happy.' Natasha, a tall woman, stared with hard challenge into his eyes.

'I should never have started with you,' he said.

A shadow fell across her blue eyes. 'You told me once you were in love with me. I'm still in love with you.'

'Why don't you get over it?' he suggested harshly.

'Easier said than done, Scotty. Don't get mad at me. I'm your friend. I've loved you far too much and far too long. You've made a big mistake getting yourself hitched up to Carrie McNevin. You haven't got a damned thing in common. And how ridiculous is that virgin bit?' Her lips curled in a sneer.

'Shut up,' Scott hissed violently, in the next minute thankful the dance music had changed to something loud and upbeat. Why had he ever told Natasha about Carrie and himself? He was a thousand times sorry.

'Watch it!' she warned, an answering rage in her eyes. 'You don't want people to see how jealous you are my cousin is fascinating your beloved little virgin. I have to admit he scrubs up pretty well. That's the Cunningham in him, of course. Why don't we sit this out for a while? Or we could go outside?'

'Forget it,' he said bluntly.

Her expression was both wounded and affronted. 'What is it she's got? I'm beautiful, too. Is it the hunt? The thrill of the chase? Once you've had her you won't want her anymore.'

'You don't understand *anything*,' Scott said, shaking his head as if to clear it. 'Carrie appeals to the best part of me. When I'm with her I remember I have a soul.'

That affected Natasha more than the cruellest rebuff. 'You fool!' she said.

Scott gave up. In the middle of the dance floor he dropped his arms from around her and walked away, leaving Natasha feeling hollowed out, gutted. Why did she love Scott Harper? It dismayed and humiliated her. She was well aware of his character flaws, which that little innocent Carrie wasn't. Living through this engagement was a long nightmare. She knew Scott had used her up—she had let him, was still letting him—but damn if he was going to throw her away. Maybe it was about time she had a little talk with darling Carrie even if she risked having her own life torn apart.

Carrie danced twice more with Clay Cunningham. It was driving Scott crazy, but he couldn't seem to do a damn thing about it. Cunningham set the pace. Other guys lined up to dance with her. He was drinking too much and he knew it. Alcohol was flowing like water from a bubbling fountain. His mind swirled with crazy thoughts.

Get Carrie on her own.

She had denied him for far too long. They were engaged now. It was his right to have her whether with her consent or not. In his experience girls said *no* all the time when what they really meant was *yes, yes, yes!* He could have any girl he wanted. Natasha Cunningham. Why did he want Carrie so desperately? There was even a strong chance she didn't go for sex. That would be a disaster. Sex was as essential for him as breathing air.

It didn't take him long to come up with an idea. He could tell her he had something for her in the SUV. A little present. Women loved being given presents, though to be honest, Carrie was no gold digger. But couldn't she feel his pain, his desire? No, she was oblivious to everything except remaining a *virgin*. Scott's anger turned ugly, a red mist swirling before his eyes. He remembered the expression on her face as she'd looked up at Cunningham. What *was* it exactly? Curiosity, a deep interest? More than that. A *craving* for something she had never had. Scott only knew she had never turned such a gaze on him. His face darkened.

Finally he had her to himself. They crossed the street with Scott holding her firmly by the arm. 'No, I won't tell you. It's a surprise!' he said in a playful voice he dredged up from somewhere.

She turned to him, puzzled. 'Why did you leave it in the car, Scott? Is it big?' She laughed a little although she was uneasy, concerned Scott had had far too much to drink. Not that he was the only one. The whole hall was filled with tipsy people, singing, dancing, chanting, full of high spirits that would last through until dawn. She couldn't worry about them but she was afraid Scott might make something of a spectacle of himself with his father around. Bradley Harper just wouldn't understand. Usually Scott held his drink well, but tonight was different. He was slurring his words. He never did that.

It was dark under the shadow of the trees that ringed the town park. The gums were smothered in blossom. There was a lovely lemony scent in the air. A little way in the distance she could see couples strolling arm in arm through the park, their bodies spotlighted by the overhead lighting. Others had moved off to cars either to catch a nap or indulge in a spot of canoodling. The big question was, why didn't she want Scott to make love to her? Saying he'd had too much to drink wasn't answer enough. She was going to marry him in three months time. My God, she should be ravenous for his lovemaking. She was so perturbed tears sprang to her eyes.

'Let's sit in the back for a moment,' Scott said, opening up the rear door and all but pushing her in.

'I don't know,' she wavered. 'We shouldn't stay.'

'You're not a bit of fun, are you?' Scott climbed in beside her, turning to her and cupping her face hard with his hand.

'What's the matter with you, Scott?' She shook her head vigorously to free his grip. 'You're in a mood.' It couldn't have been more obvious now.

'Thanks to you,' he said bitterly, abandoning all pretence.

'I've no idea what you mean!' She tried to defend herself. 'Where's the present?' She couldn't have cared less about any present. She just wanted this over.

'What do you know?' he laughed. 'I forgot to bring it with me.'

'Ah, Scott!' She tried hard to fight down her dismay.

'You don't want to be here with me, do you?' he accused her, his hot temper rising.

'Not when you're making me nervous,' she answered truthfully.

'Kiss me.' His voice grated harshly.

She could smell his damp breath, heavy with bourbon. She tried to draw away. 'We have all the time in the world for kisses. Not *here*, Scott. Our parents expect us to set a certain standard.'

'Damn them!' he said violently, getting his arms around her. 'You tell me you're a virgin, but I'm worried you're *not!* You females are full of wiles.'

He sounded terrible, hardly recognisable. A different Scott from the one she knew.

'I refuse to have this discussion now, Scott,' she said quietly, though she was starting to shake inside. 'Let's go back to the hall. Please.'

'Why don't I find out right here and now?' he responded, making his intentions very clear.

She hit him then, a cold spasm of dread causing a real ache in her stomach. It was absolutely spontaneous, her cracking slap to the side of his head. 'I don't lie, understand?' she panted. 'I demand respect from you, Scott!'

He gripped her delicate shoulders, all male force and threat. 'Now isn't that the strangest thing of all! Little Carrie McNevin attacking me.' With a grinding laugh he hauled her to him, hard and tight, crushing her body against him. 'You're *mine,* Carrie. You better believe it. I'm sick to death of holding off. Can't you feel me.' He forced her hand down to his powerful erection. 'I'm mad for you! What is making love anyway, a big mortal sin?'

He cranked up his offensive. He was half on top of her, shoving his tongue deeper and deeper into her mouth. Carrie almost gagged.

'Now we're talking!' he crowed in triumph, his hand buried in the front of her dress, his fingers clamping on to her breast. 'You're the freshest, sweetest girl in the world,' he grunted. 'You made me a promise, Carrie. You accepted my ring. Now accept *me!*'

Quick as a striking snake his other hand was under her skirt, while he rammed her body back into the seat.

'Stop, Scott. *Please.*' She was forced to beg, but she was damned if she was going to scream.

'Relax, you're going to love this.' His hungry hand was at the top of her panties.

'Dammit, I said *stop!*' Carrie cried, cursing her own stupidity. She was frightened of his brute strength. Drunk or not, he was physically in control. Even his weight was relentless. She could never get clear of him.

It was time to think, not give in. The day hadn't arrived when she was going to lie back and take it. Not like *this* anyway. This wasn't love. This was catastrophe. Rape. She let her body go slack, seemingly quiescent, as his hand plunged between her legs. He was moaning now. Moaning with a kind of fierce animal pleasure, primal in its mindlessness.

It was now or never. Carrie gathered herself, fiercely ignoring that his hand was going where it had never gone before. There wasn't much of her but she was fit. And she was an expert horse-woman with strong legs and knees. She waited her moment then when his fingers were about to thrust into her, she rammed one of her knees hard into his sensitive scrotum.

He *howled*! He actually howled! The sound was wild and appalled. Sexual passion turned to a stunned rage. 'God, you bitch!' He lifted a hand to hit her, only the contempt in her voice stopped him in his tracks.

'Don't hit me, Scott. Don't even attempt to go there.'

'You bitch!' he repeated, thinking she needed teaching a lesson. Some part of him was ashamed, the rest was in a whole lot of pain. He let out another moan, rolling across the seat away from her and hunching over, clutching his throbbing parts.

With a dazzling turn of speed Carrie was out of the SUV and on to the grass. Anger burned inside her. She tried desper-ately to straighten her clothing. What motivated men to behave the way they did? It was a very big question that had never been answered.

A voice called sharply from the other side of the street. 'You all right, Caroline?'

She could have died from humiliation. Clay Cunningham. This was a nightmare. What was she supposed to do, wave? Call out her fine handsome fiancée had just tried to rape her? 'I'm okay. It's nothing,' she answered, her mouth so dry she could barely form the words.

Clay didn't seem too impressed with that. He strode across the street, moving towards the parked vehicle. He watched in disgust as Scott Harper, holding his crotch staggered out of it. 'Mind your own bloody business, Cunningham,' Scott gritted, his voice full of hate and loathing.

'Sorry.' Clay Cunningham had made the transformation from Mr. Nice Guy to one tough looking character, powerfully intimidating. 'I'm not the kind of guy who walks away from a lady in distress. Come over here, Caroline,' he instructed.

'Don't do a damn thing he asks you,' Scott snarled her a warning.

That really bugged her. She responded by running around the front of the vehicle, clearly making her choice. When she was on her own maybe she'd have a good howl herself, but for now she had to get away from Scott. At least until he came to his senses. That she was running to Clay Cunningham was just one of life's great ironies.

'You've torn your dress,' he said, his eyes moving swiftly over her. The light from the street lamp revealed to him the stress on her delicate face. The bodice of her gown had fallen so low it disclosed the rising curves of her lovely high breasts. One of the thin straps that held it was ripped, the other fell off her shoulder. He watched her straightening it.

'I'll get her another one,' Scott lurched towards them, ready and willing to do battle. 'Why don't you get the hell away from here, Cunningham? Do you really think you're capable of stealing *my* fiancée?'

'Where do you want to go, Caroline?' Clay asked, ignoring Scott.

'I can't go back into the hall,' she said, fighting down her humiliation. She had lost one of her hair combs. She couldn't retrieve it. Not now. It would have to stay in the SUV. 'You can walk me back to the hotel if you would. I'm calling it a night.'

'Don't go, Carrie,' Scott called to her with great urgency. 'Let's start remembering *I'm* your fiancé.'

'I thought that meant I could trust you, Scott,' she retorted, as though he were beneath contempt. 'I don't want to talk about this.'

'If you walk off with *him* our engagement's finished! That's right, finished!' he shouted, as if she were about to make the worst mistake of her life.

'Then let's get it over with!' Carrie didn't go to pieces—

though she felt like it. She tugged at the diamond solitaire on her finger, then when it was off, she threw it directly at him. 'You might like to give this to Natasha. She's got a reputation for making out in cars.'

My God! For a shocked moment Scott went cold. Did Carrie *know* about him and Natasha? 'Hey, come on,' he cajoled, trying to get a grip on himself. 'Natasha means nothing to me.'

When did you find out? he wondered, but didn't dare ask.

Carrie, however, still had no idea of the secret liaison between Scott and Natasha that continued right into their engagement.

'Be careful you don't stomp on the ring,' she warned. 'It will do another turn. Good night, Scott.'

'Carrie, don't go!' He reverted to pleading as she and Cunningham began to move off. 'I love you. I've had so much to drink.'

Clay Cunningham intervened. 'There's no need for everyone to know, Harper. Keep your voice down.'

'You talkin' to *me*?' Still hurting, Scott made a maddened charge forwards, full of bravado, fists flying, ready to show Cunningham a thing or two. His mind inevitably flew back to the way he had knocked Cunningham down when they were kids. He could take him now. Cunningham was a good three inches taller, but he was heavier and he'd had years of training.

'Oh for God's sake, no!' Carrie was fearful they would soon have an audience ready to cheer a fight on. She couldn't help knowing some people would enjoy seeing Golden Boy Harper get a thrashing.

Only Clay Cunningham didn't want any fight. He threw out a defensive arm to block Scott's vicious punch. At the same time he threw a single punch of his own. It landed squarely on the point of Scott's jaw as he knew it would. Scott staggered back in astonishment, trying desperately to recover from the effects of that blow. Only his legs buckled, then went out from under him as he fell to the grass groaning afresh.

'You've hurt him,' Carrie said, in a sad and sorry voice, but not feeling encouraged to go to her ex-fiancé.

'He'll live,' Clay assured her in a clipped voice. 'The fight's over. Let's get out of here, Caroline, before we draw a crowd.'

This was a turning point for Carrie. Her life could go in one of two directions. With Scott. Or without him.

CHAPTER THREE

'So what exactly happened?' It was ten o'clock the next morning. Carrie and her mother were sitting in a quiet corner of the pub having coffee which Katie had served with some freshly baked pastries.

'I don't want to go into it, Mamma,' Carrie said carefully.

'But darling, I need to know.' Alicia leaned forward across the bench table. 'One moment you were there, the belle of the ball. Next time I looked you and Scott were gone. Did you have an argument? I wouldn't be surprised if you did. Scott has a jealous streak and you did appear to be enjoying yourself with Clay Cunningham, who incidentally, is an extraordinarily attractive young man with a strong look of his father. He disappeared as well and he didn't come back.'

'Scott and I did have a few words,' Carrie confided, unwilling to upset her mother.

Alicia frowned slightly. 'Scott's hopelessly in love with you, darling. You *are* putting him under quite a bit of pressure.'

'Are you suggesting I sleep with him, Mamma?'

Alicia glanced away. 'Who would blame you if you had that in mind? You *are* engaged. You're to be married in December.'

'So I should feel free to jump into bed? Or rather Scott should feel free to force me into sex?' Carrie took several hot, angry breaths.

'Gracious, darling, that's not what he tried to do?' Alicia looked extremely dismayed. 'Everything has been going so very well.'

Carrie began to spoon the chocolate off her coffee. 'He was drunk, Mamma. I've never seen him like that before. Losing to Clay Cunningham set him off.'

'That's one of his little failings,' Alicia said, thanking God it wasn't a whole lot worse. 'Scott's a bad loser.'

'I don't know that we should count that as a *little* failing,' Carrie said. 'In many ways Scott has been spoiled rotten. His mother idolises him—'

'Heavens, she couldn't love him more than your father and I love you.' Alicia looked at her daughter dotingly.

'Does Dad love me?' Carrie asked bleakly. *Lord, did I really say that!* 'I'd really like to know. He *wants* to love me, he tries hard to love me but it seems to place too much of a burden on him.'

'Sweetheart, you shock me. Please don't talk like that.' Alicia's beautiful eyes filled with tears. 'Your father is a very reserved man. You know that. He doesn't know how to be demonstrative. You have to take it into account.'

'I assure you I have done. For years.' Carrie couldn't let go of the mountain of pain that was inside. 'Why did you marry him? You're very different people.'

Alicia laughed shakily. 'I suppose we are.' She didn't attempt to deny it. 'But we were very much in love.'

'Well, that's good to hear. Actually Dad loves you to death! He tolerates me, because I look like you.'

Alicia's dark eyes grew wide with shock. She bowed her graceful head. 'Carrie, you're upsetting me, darling.'

'That's certainly not my intention,' Carrie reached out to take her mother's hand. 'There couldn't be many fathers who would bypass their only child—a lowly daughter—for their nephew who's nowhere near as smart as I am, could there? Alex would be the first to admit it. I'm not even sure he *wants* Victory Downs.'

Alicia's voice was heavy with irony. 'He will when he's old enough. I console myself you don't need it darling. You're going to marry Scott. You will be so well looked after. His will be a splendid inheritance.'

'*His* inheritance, not mine, Mamma,' Carrie pointed out. 'Even the Japanese government is driven to pass a law to allow the little princess to become Empress in due course.'

'And so she should!' Alicia said emphatically, when she had to all intents and purposes given up the fight to have Carrie inherit the McNevin station. 'Now regards Scott. Give him time to apologise for his less than acceptable behaviour last night. I know he will. He's mad about you, Carrie.'

'Why exactly?' Carrie asked, staring at her mother, waiting for her answer. 'It's becoming as much a mystery to me as you and Dad. Scott worked very hard to sweep me off my feet. He was determined to and he succeeded. You welcomed him as a prospective son-in-law, so did Dad. At long last I'm in Dad's good books. He's been much more relaxed with me since the engagement, hasn't he? I pleased him, made him proud. It was a good feeling. For a while.'

Alicia's hand on her coffee cup was shaking. 'Don't make any hasty decisions you might come to regret,' she warned. 'A devil gets into the best of men from time to time.'

'You sound like you know what you're talking about. Actually you sound like you led a secret life, Mamma,' Carrie said, surprised to see her mother's cheeks fill with warm colour. It was so unlike her to blush.

'My past is an open book,' Alicia declared, spreading her hands. 'I can't say I came to my marriage a virgin. You could teach me a thing or two about abstinence, my darling, but I only had one lover—before your father. When I finally got out of a Catholic boarding school there was no stopping me. I was ravishing in those days. All the boys were in love with me.'

'I bet!' The number of men who had fallen in love with her

mother was legendary, but Alicia had never been known to have affairs. That would have killed the husband who worshipped her. 'You know you're a dark horse, Mamma,' Carrie said simply. 'Who was he?' It occurred to her, her mother might have a whole host of secrets hidden away.

Alicia put her hands together as if in prayer. 'Good gracious, darling, I'm sorry I mentioned it. No one had what your father had to offer.'

'And what was that exactly? A well-respected name? Money? A historic sheep station?' Carrie asked. She couldn't say it—she didn't even want to think it—but her father could be a very boring man, given to the silent treatment.

'Not to be sneezed at,' Alicia said briskly. 'There are more important considerations than romantic love in marriage. Love is a madness anyway. And so short-lived! There's no such thing as eternal passion I'm afraid, my darling. Any fool can fall in love. It takes time and hard work to grow a successful marriage. It is a bit like gardening. Putting down good strong roots. Your father and I mightn't appear as demonstrative as other couples but we understand one another. We'll stay together.'

There had to be something about her parents' relationship she couldn't see. 'Can you imagine life without him?' Carrie asked, knowing however much she looked like her mother she had an entirely different temperament and approach to life. Where did that come from? she wondered, certainly not her father.

'What a question! This coffee is a bit strong and it's going cold. Look out for Katie. We'll order more. Your father is in splendid health. So am I.'

But Carrie persisted. 'Did Dad ever make you feel breathless with excitement? Under a spell?' There was something in her mother's eyes that was troubling her. 'Did he ever make you feel you could do something utterly rash? Be powerless to stop yourself?'

'Please…please, Carrie.' Alicia clutched the table as if the whole world had started to spin. 'The emotions you're describing can cause a lot of pain. Even ruin lives that were once full of promise. You're in a very unsettled mood aren't you, my darling girl?' she asked, worried Carrie might be thinking of calling the engagement off.

Carrie began to confirm her worst fears. 'I don't think I want to marry Scott and leave you behind,' Carrie said, staring back at her beautifully groomed mother who always looked that way. 'I've had the feeling recently he'd like to chop me off from my family. He wants me all to himself.'

Alicia stifled a deep sigh. 'And who could blame him! But that first hectic flush will pass. Your father and I will be very much in the picture. Count on it. We're looking forwards to becoming doting grandparents.'

Carrie's voice was shaky, her small face tense. 'I feel differently about Scott today,' she said, thinking of his hard, hurting hands on her body.

Concern flew into Alicia's face. 'Oh darling, give yourself a little time. He shocked you with his demands, did he?'

'He did,' Carrie said grimly.

Alicia's honeyed speaking voice turned icy cold. 'Really! Would you like your father to have a word with him?'

'God, no.' Carrie was appalled.

'It wouldn't bother me to speak to him,' Alicia said, itching to do it.

'Please, no, Mamma '

'Men aren't saints, my darling.'

'I never thought for a moment they were!' Carrie answered.

'You're a beautiful *and* sexy young woman, Carrie, even if you don't see it. In many ways you're unawakened. Of course I respect your decision to remain a virgin. Probably a very smart move with someone like Scott.'

'Smart moves had nothing to do with my decision,' Carrie pointed out, with a trace of admonition.

'Of course not. I don't really know why I said that. My advice is, if it wasn't all that bad—my God, I'm sure we're not talking rape—forgive him if you can. If you can't—' Alicia threw up her elegant hands '—your father and I will always back your decision.'

'*You* will,' Carrie said. 'I don't know about Dad. I think he'd be bitterly disappointed if I went to him and said the engagement was over.'

'But you're not going to do that, are you, darling?' More than anything Alicia wanted to see her daughter make a good marriage. Scott Harper mightn't be perfect but he had a lot going for him. 'One can understand his being in serious need of sex,' she pointed out gently.

'Be that as it may, whatever happened I dealt with it,' Carrie said. 'And Clay Cunningham came along at the right moment to back me up.'

Alicia drew in a sharp, whistling breath. 'Clay Cunningham? Now I do feel rather sorry for Scott. So Clay Cunningham rescued you like a true hero?'

Carrie on the other hand sounded suddenly *pleased*. 'He knocked Scott down.'

'Good God! I must say he had to wait a long time to do that,' Alicia laughed shortly. 'It's no secret Scott put Clay in hospital when they were boys.'

'I had no idea Scott was such a bully,' Carrie said. 'Or I didn't know until last night.' Now she sounded bitter and angry.

'You used to wave to Clay whenever you saw him in town,' Alicia suddenly recalled. 'You didn't wave to everybody.'

'He told me I used to wave,' Carrie said. 'I don't remember at all.' She didn't add she'd been trying very hard to.

'He was a handsome boy. Now a striking young man. That red in his hair he got from his mother, though she was pure

Titian. I only saw her once or twice. She was so pretty. An English rose. I wanted to befriend her but your father was very much against it. He sided with the Cunninghams. So did most people. Reece was to marry Elizabeth Campbell. It was as good as written in stone.'

'It shouldn't have been,' Carrie said, acutely aware of her own change of heart. 'You might as well know, Mamma, I gave Scott his ring back.' No need to say she had pitched it at him.

'Darling!' For one extraordinary moment there was a gleam of satisfaction in Alicia's eyes. 'He must have received one hell of a shock, being, as he is, God's gift to women. *My* only concern is for *you*. If you don't want to marry Scott Harper, there's just one thing to do. Tell him. But first give him a chance to apologise. To tell you he deeply regrets causing you pain. I'm sure he'll do just that.'

Katie appeared from the direction of the kitchen and Alicia held up her hand. 'Yoo-hoo, Katie, Carrie and I would love two more coffees. The little pastries were delicious.'

'Glad you liked 'em, Mrs. Mac!' Katie called cheerfully.

Just as her mother had predicted Scott, looking pallid beneath his tan and deeply troubled, sought out his ex-fiancée. The diamond solitaire was in his shirt pocket. No way could he let Carrie go out of his life. She was perfect. What girl ever was or would be again?

It was another brilliant day. A big barbecue lunch had been organised in the park to start at 1:00 p.m. Afterwards entertainment had been arranged for the kids, clowns and games, kites and balloons, rides on the darling little Shetland ponies and for the older, more daring kids, rides on two very aristocratic looking desert camels.

Carrie was helping out at the tables when Scott approached her. 'Carrie, could I talk to you, please?'

'It's okay, love, go right ahead. We're fine here,' one of the women on the committee called to her, giving Scott a coy wave.

'Last night was a nightmare,' Scott began wretchedly. He took Carrie's arm, drawing her along a path beneath a canopy of white flowering bauhinia trees like a bridal walk. 'I can't tell you how sorry I am any of that happened. I've been agonising about it and I reckon someone had to have spiked my drink. I've never been so out of it in my life.'

'The question is will you be out of it again?' Beautiful as the day was, sorry as Scott seemed, Carrie wasn't ready to forgive. She had come very close to being violated. Scott's assault on her had caused revulsion and a sense of inner devastation. She had trusted him. She knew it was a struggle for him no sex before marriage but she sincerely believed it was worthwhile for both of them. Her mood of desolation was further deepened by the knowledge he had been on the point of hitting her and from the look on his face, hitting her very hard. Physical violence horrified her.

'I swear by all that's holy, I'll never force myself on you again,' Scott said, sounding miserably abject. 'It was all the alcohol, Carrie. That and seeing you in Cunningham's arms. It drove me right off the edge.'

'Why exactly?' Carrie asked. 'We were enjoying a dance in front of hundreds of people. You didn't catch us in some compromising position.'

'It was the look on your face,' Scott said. 'It had a closeness about it you never give me.'

'Nonsense,' Carrie said firmly, though she felt herself under scrutiny. 'You're a frighteningly jealous person. Now I think about it, a domineering sort of man.' *Like your father,* hung in the air.

'What is it, Carrie?' Scott groaned. 'You need me to be perfect? Near inhuman? I'm madly in love with you. I'm a man of twenty-nine, nearly thirty, and you don't want me to touch you? Do you know how hard that is?'

'Yes, I do,' she said quietly, her reaction to Clay Cunningham taking over her mind, 'but I was proud of your sense of discipline, your consideration of my wishes.'

'You can't forgive me for *one* mistake?' Scott just stopped himself from turning ugly.

'That one mistake showed me you're not the man I thought you were,' Carrie said, brushing a spent white bauhinia blossom from her shoulder. 'You were even going to hit me. Don't deny it. You were going to slap me very hard. That was *bad*, Scott. Is that what you do when a woman doesn't give consent?'

'Oh God, Carrie!' Scott's voice was a heartfelt lament. 'I wouldn't really have hit you. I think maybe I thought about it for half a second.'

'Wrong. You were about to do it. Somehow I was able to stop you. Perhaps it was the disgust in my voice.'

Quite simply it had been. 'Carrie, I can't really remember last night,' he said. 'I can't be certain I hadn't been given some drug.'

'Did you take something?' She glanced up at him, knowing there was nowhere designer drugs hadn't reached.

'Carrie, stop punishing me,' he said. 'I love you. I'm desperate to marry you. I'll never deliberately cause you pain again. I beg you. Give me one more chance.' His eyes were extraordinarily intense. 'Is that too much to ask of the girl who's supposed to love me? You can't abandon me for one mistake.'

'Two bad mistakes.'

'We're getting married in December,' Scott pressed on. 'I've tried. God, how I've tried!'

This at least was true. Despite herself Carrie found herself moved by his obvious pain and contrition. 'Oh, Scott,' she sighed in a dispirited kind of way. She had a big problem now deciding she had ever loved him. A problem that hadn't really existed before Clay Cunningham came back into their lives.

'Please, darling.' Scott fumbled for the diamond solitaire in his pocket. 'A commitment has been made, Carrie. We can sort this out. Everyone is so happy we're together. My parents, your parents. Your dad and I are good mates. He thoroughly approves me of as a son-in-law.'

Wasn't that the truth! An outsider if asked might have said Scott was Bruce McNevin's offspring rather than his daughter.

'Let me prove to you all over again how much I love you,' Scott said ardently, lifting her hand and pushing his ring home on her finger. 'I'm nothing without you.' He lifted her hand to his mouth and kissed it tenderly. 'Say you forgive me.'

Carrie shook her head. 'That's impossible for me to say today, Scott.' She had never felt so dejected, so unsure of herself to the point of tears.

'It's your father. He's coming towards us,' Scott told her swiftly, seeing Bruce McNevin hurrying towards them across the grass. 'Don't let me down.'

'Ah, there you are, you two!' Bruce McNevin, having witnessed that heart-warming little moment between Carrie and Scott, called to them in a voice that was almost affectionate. A big concession for him. 'I've organised a corner table for all of us near the fountain. Your mother and father, Scott, Alicia and I and you two lovebirds.' He eyed them both with wry amusement. 'Goodness, from the look of you both, you must have been up all night.'

'Darn nearly sir.' Scott flashed his prospective father-in-law a respectful smile. 'Thanks for organising the table. I can tell you we're definitely hungry.'

Clay stayed in town for three reasons: as the winner of the Jimboorie Cup; to get to know people; and to avail himself of the magnificent barbecue lunch free to all. Or so he told himself. Why he *really* stayed was to keep a watchful eye on Caroline. She had well and truly aroused his protective streak which was always near the surface when it came to vulnerable women. Now he wanted to see how she was going to handle an ex-fiancé who was determined to fight his way back into her good books.

The worst of it was, Harper appeared to have succeeded. Though Clay did his best not to look too often in their direction he had noted Caroline was not only wearing her big solitaire again, but Harper was sitting close beside her, in the company of both sets of smiling parents. As to be expected theirs was the best table set under the trees near the playing fountain.

Last night he had escorted Caroline back to Dougherty's pub where she was staying. He had asked if she were okay, then when she said she was, he said a quiet good-night watching her walk up the stairs to the guest bedrooms. He had longed to stay. To offer a few words of comfort—he had even wanted to rush into some good advice—but he could see how upset and vulnerable she was. The torn skirt of her beautiful dress and the ripped shoulder strap made him so angry he felt like going back outside to find Harper and give him the thrashing he deserved.

Caroline wouldn't thank him for that. She wanted the incident kept as quiet as possible. It was quite a miracle they had made it back to the pub without anyone paying them any particular attention. Caroline had tucked the torn shoulder strap into her bodice and her skirt was long and swishy concealing the rent. Such damage spoke for itself.

Harper had attacked her. Attacked the young woman he professed to love—his wife-to-be! Child, and man, Harper was a born bully. And what was it about anyway? Obviously Harper had wanted to make love to her—just as obviously she had said no. Any man in his right mind would have accepted it. Harper, alcohol driven, had nevertheless revealed the inner man. He had forced her only in this case he had underestimated his fiancée's fighting qualities. A woman at bay, even a pocket-sized one, could inflict damage if she were able to overcome her fear and get in a telling kick where it hurt most.

Clay felt proud of her. Like a big brother. Best to think of it like that. After all she'd used to wave to him from when she was a toddler until she was about six. And what a beautiful little girl she had been.

For another two hours he had sat across the street from the pub keeping an eye on the entrance just in case Harper took it into his mind to try to get Caroline alone again. He hadn't showed, though Clay was struck by the fact at one point in the night he had seen Harper in the distance having what looked like a serious disagreement with his cousin, Natasha. Impossible to miss her tall, willowy figure and the light was shining on her violet dress. Natasha might have been his cousin, but she wanted no part of Clay. On the other hand, why had Natasha been engaged in a violent argument with Harper? She couldn't have been acting on Caroline's behalf. Clay had gained the strong impression during the course of the afternoon and evening Caroline and Natasha weren't at all friendly. Yet a strong link existed between Natasha and Harper. How else could both of them have been filled with such anger? Clay had to admit he found that troubling.

Surrounded by 'family' Carrie was feeling hemmed in. She was tormented by her complex emotions. Had she really agreed to give Scott a second chance? She didn't think so, yet why was she seated at this table as if nothing had happened? Her mother had given her a quick, surprised glance after registering the diamond solitaire was back on her finger. Alicia didn't say anything but she patted Carrie's arm gently. Two lovers had had a fight and made up. It was much easier not to rock the boat. Alicia was in excellent spirits as was her father.

Why am I doing this? Carrie wondered. Was she in such desperate need of her father's approval? The deep reserve of his lifelong manner with her, the distancing, the lack of response, had caused her much grief and pain. She was sure that was why her mother had sent her away to boarding school early. Her mother gave her plenty of love and affection, cared for her as a mother should, but it was never enough. Her mother told her pretty much daily, 'I love you.' Her father—and she had racked her memory—had *never* said it. Surely that was wrong, wrong, *wrong!* Instead of disturbing her less, it disturbed her more and more as she grew older. It suddenly occurred to her, before her engagement to Scott Harper her existence hadn't had much significance for her father. Now with blinding clarity she saw that her father's approval rated higher than Scott's love.

That was immensely disturbing.

Across the green parkland she glimpsed Clay Cunningham seated at a table with the very attractive McFadden sisters, Jade and Mia. They were really sweet girls. The whole family was nice. The sisters sat on either side of him looking thrilled to be there. Several other young people she knew, including the girls' younger brother Aidan, made up the number at the table. If Clay Cunningham was desperate to find himself a bride he had arrived in town at the optimum time. It would be another year before the town saw such a gathering. As she expected, given Clay Cunningham was such a stunning man, both sisters were flushed with excitement as was Susie Peterson of the big blue eyes sitting opposite him. Susie leaned across the table to say something to him, which made them all laugh.

Carrie almost laughed herself. No need to help him out with his Bush Bachelor advertisement. He actually had three eligible young women hanging on his every word. If he were serious about finding a bride he'd better make the most of this glorious opportunity. After today they would all go their separate ways; home to pastoral properties all over the vast State. Distance was a big factor in the difficulties confronting those wanting to form meaningful relationships. Distance and back breaking sunup to sundown hard work that left precious little time for play.

After lunch Carrie helped out with the children's races. Even if she said so herself she had a talent with kids. They always welcomed her around. Afterwards she took a turn leading the little ones mounted on Shetland ponies around the sandy oval, the ponies perfectly behaved if not the kids. It was good to be able to make her escape from the 'family.' Though she had tried her hardest she'd found lunchtime oppressive. Once she had caught Scott's mother, Thea, looking at her with an odd expression in her eyes. A kind of what's-going-on-here? Mrs Harper's enmity would be deadly if she decided to go ahead and call off the engagement.

To her surprise she saw Clay Cunningham take a turn at leading around the older kids in saddlelike rigs aboard the camels. These domesticated camels came from a Far West property. Camels were such intelligent animals, Carrie thought. Not indigenous to the continent, they had been brought to Australia along with their Afghan handlers in the early days of settlement. Camels had been used on the ill-fated Burke and Wills expedition, by other explorers, miners, telegraph line builders, surveyors, station owners, tradesmen of all kinds. Camels had been *the* beasts of burden all over the Outback. Now they numbered around three hundred thousand, the healthiest camels on the planet. To Carrie's mind their heavy, long lashed eyelids gave them a benign look but she knew in the wild they could be dangerous.

There was no danger today. The camels couldn't have been more docile and obliging. They didn't even mind the excited little sidekicks they were getting from the children, predictably the boys, to spur them on. She was reminded how Scott had used his whip on Sassafras when Clay Cunningham had 'talked' his horse home.

She had a breather from Scott. He had gone off with her father to try their hand at flying the big, wonderfully painted and decorated kites too difficult for youngsters to handle. She could see one swooping up and up in the sky. It really had been a flawless day.

Aidan McFadden approached her, giving her a big smile. 'I'll take over from you now, Carrie. You must feel like a rest from this lot?'

'I sure do.' Carrie returned the smile. 'A cold drink will go down well. Thanks, Aidan. It's been a great weekend, hasn't it?'

'As far as I'm concerned the new guy Clay Cunningham put on the best show. Boy can he ride!' Aidan's open expression registered admiration. 'Do you think he'd mind if I took a look at the old homestead sometime? I was going to ask him. He sat at our table for lunch. He's a nice, easygoing guy. Do you really think he will stay? I hope he will. Only old Angus Cunningham left Jimboorie in a woeful state.'

'He had a breakdown after his wife died,' Carrie said. 'Then his daughter left him. He was a sad, sad man. Clay told me he wants to stay, Aidan. Why don't you simply ask him if you can visit sometime? Unless he's disappeared.' She glanced around the area.

'No, he's still around.' Aidan grinned. 'He can't shake Jade and Mia. Is it true he's looking for a wife? Or is that a bit of a joke? We didn't like to ask him but I can tell you the girls want him for themselves.'

'He can only pick one.' Carrie smiled back, but she felt a prick of something very much like misery.

'Then it's Jade!' Aidan called hopefully after her.

Clay Cunningham had won the McFaddens over it seemed.

One of the committee ladies met her with a home-made lemonade in a tall frosted glass decorated with a sprig of mint. 'Thank you so much, Carrie. You're always such a help. The kids love you.'

'I love them,' Carrie answered truthfully, accepting the very welcome drink. 'Where's Mamma?'

'Talking to Thea Harper the last time I saw her. The wedding's not far off now. You'll make the most beautiful bride,' she gushed.

Carrie smiled but could not answer. Was it possible she was having the first of a sequence of panic attacks?

'Hi, Caroline!' a deep attractive male voice called. A voice she now thought she'd know anywhere.

She paused, turning her head. 'Hello there, Clay.'

'How are you today?' He caught up to her, the both of them moving spontaneously towards an empty park bench.

'Very unsettled,' she admitted, sinking gratefully onto the timber seat.

'I couldn't help noticing Harper is forgiven.' He glanced down at her slender, polished fingers. The diamond solitaire was blazing away in a chink of sunlight.

'Everyone is just so happy we're engaged,' she said.

He knit his mahogany brows. 'Everyone but you.'

She risked a direct glance into his face, bewilderment surging into her voice. 'I used to be happy. Or I thought I was. Maybe I was just basking in everyone's approval.'

'What does that mean exactly?' The question was intense, far from light.

'God you know all about approval and the lack of it, Clay,' she said raggedly. 'I can't talk about it. It's disloyal to my family.'

'What about Harper?' he asked in a taut low voice. 'Hell, Caroline, you're not a schoolgirl. You're a woman. What are you afraid of? You weren't afraid last night. You were astonishingly gutsy. What's happened to change that?'

She didn't answer for a moment. She took a long draft of the lemonade, moving her tongue into a curl. It was delicious and refreshingly cold. 'I was very angry with Scott last night. I'm still not happy about him, but he came to me this morning and—'

'Swore he'd never use force on you again?' he interjected. 'You believed him?'

She had the strong impression he was disgusted. 'May I ask why it's any of your business, Clay?'

'You may ask but I might be less inclined to answer.' He gave a humourless laugh. 'Think of it as I'm catching up with a friendship that never had a chance to get started. I was a pretty lonely kid, living on the fringe of things. My father dishonoured by his own people. My mother spoken about as if she were nothing more than a wayward little tramp. In reality she had more class than any of them. But it broke her as time went on. It might seem like a small thing but I saw the way little Princess McNevin always gave me a wave as a bright spot in my blighted childhood.'

'I can't remember.' She stared at him out of sorrowful doe eyes.

'Sounds like you've been trying?' His voice had a tender but challenging note.

'I know I *will* remember,' she said, clinging to the idea. 'It's going to happen all at once.'

'When can you come to Jimboorie?' he asked, with some urgency because Caroline was never on her own for long.

'It's not a good idea.' In fact it could cost her a good deal.

'Caroline, you *promised*,' he reminded her, his eyes a blazing blue against the bronze cast of his skin.

'Scott hates you.'

His handsome face bore an expression of indifference. 'That's okay. I can live with it. I don't exactly admire him. He's a bully. Man and boy. What days do you come into town for Pat Kennedy?'

She could see he wasn't going to let this alone. If the truth be told she badly wanted to accept his invitation. 'Make it next Friday,' she said. 'I'll meet you at the *Bulletin* office at 10:00 a.m. Would that suit?'

'No, but I'll be there.' He gave her a smile that made a lick of fire run right down to her toes.

'Then another day?' she suggested quickly.

He shook his head, his thick mahogany hair, lit by rich red tones. 'Friday's fine. The sooner the better. Are you going to tell your folks?'

She laughed as if it were an insane thing to ask. 'Oh, Clay, they won't even notice I've gone. Well, my father won't.'

He wanted to touch her cheek but he knew he shouldn't. 'What's the problem with your father? There appears to be one.'

'Maybe I'll tell you sometime,' she said. 'Oh, God!' she muttered, under her breath. 'Here he comes now with Scott.'

Clay rose immediately to his impressive height. 'Don't panic, I'll go. You will turn up?'

She trembled and he saw it. 'Yes. 10:00 a.m. at the office,' she repeated.

'What I'd really like to do is stay and meet your father. Ask him why he turned against the man who was once his friend?'

'Now's not the time for it, Clay!' She looked at him with a plea in her eyes.

'Don't walk into the trap,' he warned, touching a forefinger to his temple before striding away.

CHAPTER FOUR

THEY had been driving for well over an hour. There hadn't been much conversation between them, rather an intense *awareness* that made any comment deeper than normal, a potential mine-field. She had not removed her engagement ring. She offered him no explanation and he didn't ask for one, yet she carried the conviction he would before the day was over.

She'd told her mother where she was going…

'Darling, is that wise?' Alicia had shown a level of concern, bordering on alarm.

'Wise or not I'm going,' Carrie had replied. 'I really want to see the old house. When I was little I thought it was a palace like the Queen lived in.'

'And you want to see Clay Cunningham.' Alicia didn't beat about the bush.

'I like him,' Carrie said. What she failed to say was he had an extraordinary effect on her. It was something she had to keep secret. Even from herself, but Alicia's expression suggested she knew all the same.

There was Jimboorie House rising up before them. Once the cultural hub of a vast region, it stood boldly atop a rise that fell away rather steeply to the long curving billabong of Koona Creek

at its feet. It was to Carrie, far and away the most beautiful homestead ever erected by the sheep barons who became the landed
gentry. It was certainly the biggest, built of sandstone that had
weathered to a lovely soft honey-pink. It lofted two tall storeys
high, the broad terrace beneath the deep overhang of the upper
level supported by imposing stone columns, which were all but
obscured by a rampant tangle of vines all in flower. The great roof
was tiled with harmonising grey slate that had been imported all
the way from Wales. The whole effect was of an establishment
that would be considered quite impressive in any part of the
world, if only one narrowed one's eyes and totally ignored the
decay and the grime.

The mansion was approached by a long driveway guarded by
sentinel towering gums. This in turn opened out into a circular
driveway with a once magnificent fountain, now broken, in the
centre. The gardens, alas, were no more but the indestructible bou-
ganvilleas climbed over every standing structure in sight. A short
flight of stone steps led to the imposing pedimented Ionic portico.

Clay drove his 4WD into the shade of the flowering gums, the
low trailing branches scraping the hood.

'What it once must have been!' Carrie sighed. 'It's still beautiful even if it's falling down.'

'Come see for yourself,' he invited, with a note in his voice
that made her doubly curious.

Carrie stepped out onto the gravelled driveway, a petite young
woman wearing a white knit tank top over cropped cotton drill
olive-green pants, a simple wardrobe she somehow made glamorous. Their arrival disturbed a flock of rainbow lorikeets that had
been feeding on the pollen and nectar in the surrounding euca-
lypts, bauhinias, and cassias all in bloom. The birds displayed all
the colours of the spectrum in their plumage, Carrie thought, following their flight. The upper wings were emerald-green, under
wings orange washed with yellow, beautiful deep violet heads,

scarlet beaks and eyes. They presented a beautiful sight, chattering shrilly to one another as they flew to another feeding site.

A sprightly breeze had blown up, tugging at her hair which she had tied back at the nape with a silk scarf designed by aboriginal women using fascinating traditional motifs. 'What does it feel like to be back?' she asked him, filled for a moment with a real sadness for what might have been.

'Like I've never been away,' Clay answered simply, though his face held myriad emotions. 'This is precisely the place I belong.'

'Is it?' His words touched her deeply. She looked across at his tall, lean figure. He was dressed simply as she was, in everyday working clothes—tight fitting jeans, and a short sleeved open necked bush shirt. Dark, hand tooled boots on his feet gave him added stature. He had a wonderful body, she thought, starting to fear the effect he had on her. At her deepest level she knew a man like this could push over all her defences as easily as one could push over a pack of cards. It was something entirely new in her life. She wondered could she resist *him* as she was so able to resist Scott? At heart, she was beginning to question herself. Was her decision to remain a virgin until marriage brought about by sheer circumstance? It seemed very obvious to her now she didn't love Scott in the way a woman should love the man she chooses to marry. Everyone else saw him as a solid choice. Did that automatically make for a good marriage?

As for Clay Cunningham? She didn't have a clue where their friendship would lead. In short he presented a dilemma. Carrie's nerves stretched taut as her memory was overrun by images of her father and Scott as they joined her yesterday only moments after Clay had moved off. Both handsome faces wore near identical expressions. Anger to the point of outrage. It chilled her to the bone. She wasn't a possession, a chattel. She was a grown woman with the right to befriend anyone she so chose.

Her father didn't think so and made that plain. 'Better you

don't have anything to do with him, Carrie,' he'd clipped off, his grey eyes full of ice.

'Why not?' She had never in her life answered her father quite like that before. A clear challenge that brought hot, angry colour to his cheeks.

'I wouldn't have thought I had to tell you,' he reprimanded her. 'He's bad news. Just like his father before him. You're an engaged woman yet it's quite obvious he has his eye on you.'

She had waited for Scott to intervene but he hadn't. Best not get on the wrong side of Mr McNevin. At least until he and Carrie were safely married.

'That's carrying it a bit far, Dad,' Carrie had said. 'Clay just came across to say hello. I like him.'

Her father looked pained. 'People talk, Carrie. I don't want them to be talking about *you.*'

'You're very quiet today, Scott?' She hadn't bothered to hide the taunt. 'Nothing to add?'

He shook his golden head. 'As far as I'm concerned your father has said it all.'

That earned him Bruce McNevin's nod of approval.

Clay took her arm as they climbed the short flight of steps to the portico and on to the spacious terrace. 'Careful,' he said, indicating the deep gouges between the slate tiles. 'Just stay with me.'

Guilt swept through her. *Why, why, why did she want so much to be with him?* This was all too sudden. She had the mad notion she would have gone with him had he asked her to take a trip to Antarctica.

The double front doors towered a good ten feet. They were very impressive and in reasonably good condition. When she had *really* looked from the outside, she had seen the large numbers of broken or displaced tiles on the roof and the smashed glass in the tall arched windows of the upper level. Some of the shutters, once a Venetian green, were hanging askew. Panels of glass in the French doors of the lower level were broken as well and replaced with cardboard.

The effect was terrible. Some of the damage could have been caused by vandals. The smashed glass in the doors and windows for example. Six months had elapsed since Angus Cunningham's death and the arrival of his great-nephew. It could have happened then although the talk in the town was Jimboorie House was haunted by the late Isabelle Cunningham. No one had the slightest wish to encounter her.

Clay opened one door, then the other, so that long rays of sunlight pierced the grand entrance hall.

As far as Carrie was concerned, the entrance hall said it all about a house. 'Oh!' she gasped, as she stepped across the threshold. She stared about her with something approaching reverence. 'I've always wanted to see inside. It s as noble as I knew it would be.'

Her face held so much fascination it was exquisite! Clay thought. 'I'm glad you're here, and you're not disappointed.'

Something in his tone made Carrie's heart turn a somersault in her breast. She didn't look back at him—she didn't dare—but continued to stare about her. After the mess of broken tiles on the terrace she was thrilled to see the floor of the entrance hall, tessellated with richly coloured tiles was intact. In three sections, the design was beautiful, circular at the centre with equally beautiful borders.

'What a miracle it hasn't been damaged.'

'The house isn't in any where near as bad condition as everyone seems to think,' Clay commented with a considerable amount of satisfaction. 'Which is not to say a great deal of money won't be spent on its restoration.'

She stood in the sunbeams with dust motes of gold. 'It would be wonderful to hear your great-uncle actually left you some money?'

'He had it,' Clay said, surprising her.

'He couldn't have!' Carrie was completely taken aback. 'How could he have had money and let the homestead fall into ruin let alone allow the station to become so rundown?'

'He no longer cared,' Clay told her, shrugging. 'Simple as that. He cared about no one and nothing. He only loved one person in his entire life. That was his wife. After she died he slowly sank into a deep depression. She's supposed to haunt the place, incidentally. My mother claimed to have seen her many times. Isabelle died early. Thirty-eight. No age at all! I wouldn't like to think I only had another ten years of life. She was carrying Angus's heir who died with his mother. Their daughter, Meredith, the firstborn, spent most of her time at boarding school, or with her maternal aunt in Sydney who, thank the Lord, loved her. Meredith was never close to her father after her mother died. No one was. Uncle Angus locked everyone out.'

'Yet he took you in? You and your parents?'

'It was only to spite the rest of the family, I assure you,' Clay said, the hard glint of remembrance in his eyes. 'My father worked like a slave for little more than board for us all. Angus kept my father at it by telling him he was going to inherit Jimboorie. Meredith didn't want the place. Mercifully she married well. Her aunt saw to that. When Angus finally admitted he fully intended to sell up, my father decided it was high time to move on.'

'What happened to your father?' Carrie asked, positioning herself out of the dazzling beam of light so she could see him clearly.

His face became a tight mask. 'He was helping to put out a bushfire, only he and the station hand working with him became surrounded by the flames.'

'Oh, Clay!' Carrie whispered, absolutely appalled. No one knew this. At least she hadn't heard anything of Reece Cunningham's dreadful fate. 'How horrible! Why should anyone have to die like that?'

The corners of his handsome mouth turned down. 'To save the rest of us I suppose. I had to concentrate on his heroism or go mad. My mother spent the rest of her life having ghastly nightmares. The way my father died left her not only bereft but sunk in a depressive state she couldn't fight out of. That fire destroyed her, too. I know she actually prayed for the day she would die. She truly believed she would see my father again.'

'Do *you?*' she asked with a degree of trepidation.

'No.' Abruptly he shook his burnished head. 'Still I can't help but wonder from time to time.'

'Mystery, mysteries, the *great* mystery,' she said. She lifted her head to the divided staircase. Of polished cedar and splendid workmanship it led to the richly adorned overhanging gallery. The gallery had to have a dome because natural light was pouring in. Either that or there was a huge hole in the roof. The plaster ceilings, that once would have been so beautiful, were badly in need of repair.

'Does the gallery have a dome?' she asked, hoping the answer was yes.

'It does,' he said, 'and it's still intact. The bedrooms are upstairs of course. Twelve in all. The old kitchens and the servants' quarters are the buildings at the rear of the house. We'll get to them. Let's move on. There are forty rooms in the house all up.' He extended his arm to the right.

More tall double doors gave on to the formal dining room on their left, the drawing room to their right. Neither room was furnished. The drawing room was huge and classically proportioned. The once grand drapes of watered Nile-green silk were hanging in tatters.

She was both appalled and moved by the badly neglected state of the historic homestead. 'Where do you plan to start first?'

she asked, her clear voice echoing in the huge empty spaces. 'Or are you going to leave that to your wife?'

'I'll have to,' he said, amusement in his voice. 'I'll be too busy getting the station up and running.'

'So what are you going to run?' Her voice lifted with interest.

'A lean commercial operation geared for results,' he answered promptly. 'Jimboorie's glamour days are over. Beef is back. There's a strong demand. I'm going to run Hereford cattle. Angus couldn't envisage any other pursuit than running sheep even when the wool industry was in crisis.'

'Are you going to tell me where you acquired your skills as a cattleman?'

He nodded. 'I actually got to Agricultural College where I did rather well. Then I worked on a cattle station rising to overseer.'

'Would I know this station?'

'Oh, come on, Caroline,' he gently taunted her. 'You would if I told you.'

'So you think if you confide in me I'll tell everyone else?' She was hurt he didn't trust her but she made a huge effort to hide it.

'I don't think that at all. Not if I told you not to. It's just that it's difficult to talk about a lot of things right now.'

She turned away from him. 'That's okay. It's not as if we're *friends.*'

'It's not easy to make a true friend,' he said sombrely. 'What *are* we exactly?'

'We're in the process of becoming friends,' she bravely said.

'So you'd befriend me and rebuff your fiancé? It's back on again, I take it?' His tone was sardonic, if not openly critical.

'It's just a mess, Clay,' she said, that tone getting to her.

His brilliant blue eyes seemed to *burn* over her, making her skin flush. 'Well you can't disregard it. It's your life's happiness that's on the line. Are you so afraid of increasing the discord between yourself and your father?' he asked with considerable perception. 'He's obviously an extremely difficult man to please?'

She glanced away through the French doors at the abandoned garden. The wildflowers, shrubs and flowering vines that had survived lent it colour as did the hardiest of climbing cabbage roses, a magnificent deep scarlet, in full bloom over an old pergola. She had seen many pictures of Jimboorie House in its prime so she knew there had been a wonderful rose arbour. 'My father is difficult about some things,' she answered at length. 'He's a good father in others. I don't know why I'm telling you. I feel I know you.'

'You do know me,' he replied. 'You're the little girl who used to deliver the sweetest smile and the wave of a little princess, remember?'

'May I ask you a personal question?' She turned to face him, held fast by the extraordinary intensity of his gaze.

'You can try.' He smiled. 'And what would it be? Have I ever been in love?' His voice held amusement.

It wasn't her question, but she stared back at him, aware she badly wanted to know. 'Have you?'

'Caroline, I told you.'

That smile was *magic*. Few smiles lit up a man's face like that.

'My lifestyle left very little time for romance,' he explained again. 'There was a girl once. She got spooked by my lack of money. All she had to do was give me a little time.'

'Do you still love her?' The muscles in her slender throat tensed. She told herself it would be wonderful to have a man like Clay Cunningham love her. Something she knew she would agonize over later.

'No.'

'Are you sure?'

'Absolutely positive,' he said. He didn't tell her, nor would he, he'd already dated falling in love from the moment he'd laid eyes

on her, albeit rashly. He had already discovered she was the
fiancée of Scott Harper, the bully boy of his childhood. Still
was, for that matter. She wore Harper's ring. Maybe the death of
his mother and returning to Jimboorie had put him in a very vulnerable state of mind. That's why he wanted a wife, a wife and
children, a family of his own to love. Having a family of his own
had somehow developed into a passion. Caroline McNevin could
too easily become a passion. A *doomed* passion. Unless she
found the strength to break away from Harper.

Carrie moved on. 'I love the fireplace,' she said. The chimney
piece was constructed of flawless white Carrara marble. Instead
of the usual large gilded mirror to hang above it—any mirror
would probably have been shattered—was a very elegant over-
mantel in the same white marble. Judging from the staining left
on the marble, it seemed a painting had once hung there and on
other places around the walls.

'It would take a great deal of furniture to fill this room alone,'
she marvelled, finding it easy to visualise the drawing room
restored. She loved houses; beautiful houses like this. Clay was
quite correct in saying the interior wasn't in any where near as bad
condition as everyone thought. At least as much as she had seen.

'A lot of the original furnishings, paintings, rugs, objets d'art,
you name it, are in storage,' he said, further surprising her.

'Really?' Her dark eyes opened wide. 'On the property, you
mean? One of the outbuildings?'

He shook his head. 'Great-Uncle Angus wasn't so steeped in
grief he didn't make sure nothing of real value was left here to
be stolen. There's a warehouse full of it in Toowoomba.' He
named a city one hundred miles west of Brisbane, the state
capital, lying on the edge of the Great Dividing Range and
famous for its spring carnival of flowers.

'I think you could safely say your great-uncle Angus fooled
the world,' she said wryly. 'Have you seen what's in there?'

'Not as yet, but I have the inventory. I'll make the trip to Too-woomba some time fairly soon. Want to come?'

'Aren't you the bush bachelor looking for a wife?' She gave him a look.

'Most definitely,' he retorted. 'We could talk about what I should put in my ad along the way.'

'You have a devil in you, Clay Cunningham.'

He absorbed her slowly with his eyes. 'Most men do, but *you'll* never stumble on mine, I promise. You speak of loving Harper, but I don't think you do.'

She had learned that in stages. 'Off-limits, Clay,' she warned moving into the huge handsome room that was obviously the library. Cedar bookcases were set in arcaded recesses all around the room, but the collection had gone. A book lover, she prayed it had gone into storage.

'Perhaps you're a little too accustomed to doing what you believe will please everyone?' he questioned, his voice resonat-ing with a certain sympathy.

'Is that a good reason to get married?' She felt wounded.

'It happens a lot,' he said. 'I had no difficulty sensing you badly need to please your father. That desire must be far from new.'

She stopped abruptly. 'You sense far too much. What is it you want from me, Clay?' Without meaning for it to happen—her momentary weakness shocked her—tears filled her eyes.

He stared down at her in dismay. 'Caroline, don't do that,' he implored, slowly rubbing a hand across his tanned forehead. 'I've got plenty of self-control, but your tears might prove my undoing.' In reality he saw himself on the very edge of a yawning chasm. If those tears spilled onto her cheeks, he might plunge into that chasm, taking her with him, his arms enclosing her, cradling her, his mouth closing over hers to muffle her cries.

Oh God, Caroline, stop it! When he was with her his every perception was intensified.

'Meaning what?' She tried valiantly to blink the tears away.

'You know perfectly well what I mean.' His handsome face was grim. 'Why do your eyes contain tears anyway? They're no protection against me. The reverse is true. It seems to me you want to cry from sheer necessity. You're unhappy. You feel caught in a trap. You can get out of it if you're strong.'

Was she strong? She'd thought she was. Now she turned her head away from him and the tremendous temptation he presented. 'It's impossible overnight.' Her hands were shaking. She lifted one to clasp the silk scarf at her nape. She pulled it free, suddenly irritated by the knot of material on her neck.

'No, it's not,' he answered roughly, watching her hair uncoil into long golden skeins. It radiated light like a halo around her head. He couldn't help himself. He moved nearer, lifting a hand and curling a long shining lock around his fingers. It felt like silk, sweetly scented. He tugged on the thick lock very gently edging her towards him.

'Don't *do* this, Clay,' she warned, knowing they had both reached a turning point that was far from unexpected.

'Look into my eyes and tell me that,' he said. His hand moved to the mass of her shining hair pulling her head back so he could stare into her face. 'Caroline?'

'I must be mad,' she murmured.

'I know. So am I.'

Now the tears did seep from her eyes. What she saw in his face was sexual ardour of a nature she had hitherto never even glimpsed. It wasn't crude lust. Lust she had come to despise. There was real *yearning* there, as though he believed she might be the one to cure his deep-seated griefs. She, in turn, was spellbound by the concentration of pure desire that burned so brilliantly in his blue eyes.

She didn't so much go along with it. She surrendered herself to it, deferring to a stolen moment in time. 'This may well be a serious mistake!' The streams of passion that stormed through her veins offered proof.

He nodded solemnly, one hand cupping her face with a tenderness that was profoundly moving. 'You're so small!'

'I'm a woman,' she said. 'A woman of nearly twenty-four.'

'A very serious young woman who has to put a few things right.'

'That's how you see it?' she whispered, her eyes on his clean cut mouth.

'Don't *you*?'

Before she had time to react—did she really have the strength?—he lifted her as though she weighed no more than a child and carried her to one of the recessed alcoves, setting her on top of the solid cedar cupboard, which supported the ceiling-high bookshelves.

'Caroline McNevin, you are *so* beautiful!' He trailed one hand down over her cheek, her throat, lightly skimmed the low-necked front of her tank top that gave a tantalizing glimpse of the upward curves of her breasts.

Her body ached. There was pain, she was learning, in desire. 'Why are we doing this, Clay?'

'It's all I've wanted to do since you walked back into my life,' he confessed.

Her eyes were very dark, her expression strange. 'When kissing me is strictly forbidden?'

'By whom?'

'God help me, not *me*!'

Her words chimed in his mind. He lowered his head, while Carrie closed her eyes, dizzy suddenly with the level of sensuality.

His powerful, lean body stood directly in front of her. Without thought—all she wanted was to get as close to him as possible—she brought up her slender legs to wrap him around. It was something she had never done before but her inhibitions were melting like a polar thaw. Her fall from grace—the full rush of it—

stunned her. If indeed fall was what it was. But she had promised to marry another man, for all the decision to make a clean break from Scott was fast overtaking her.

She could pay heavily for this moment out of time. They *both* could. But Carrie was powerless to stop what had already started. The sense of having been caught up in something far beyond the power of either of them to control was strong in her. Fate, destiny, something preordained?

Gently, so *gently* at first, he touched his mouth to hers. A communion. Yet the effect was so overwhelming it drowned her in a wave of the most voluptuous heat. She had never experienced such a powerful sexual reaction. It caught at her breath so it emerged as a moan.

'I'm not hurting you?' He drew back a little.

'*No!*'

The flame and the urgency of their coming together seemed to devour her. No flutter of conscience troubled her then. His kiss was so deep and so passionate there was no question of denying him what he sought to take from her. No question of denying herself such excitement, such a tremendous physical exhilaration.

She had never dreamed a kiss could be like this.

Never!

At that dangerous moment she was his for the taking. She was *pressing* herself against him with absolute abandon. All the world was lost to her. Instead of her habitual ingrained caution she felt only a magnificent generosity. She was offering herself, shamelessly, ultimately inciting him to take as much as he wanted from her. She was acutely aware he was powerfully aroused but she had no thought of withdrawing herself or calling a stop. Desire such as this was a revelation. It was the most potent of all intoxications and she was drinking it from his mouth.

Why would she call a halt to such a storm of wanting? For all she knew it might never happen again.

'Caroline!' He gasped out her name, getting one hand to her hair that was tumbling all around them in golden sheets.

She realised with a shock he was trying to hold her off.

Oh, God!

Absolute bliss turned to blinding mortification.

His dark head was bent over hers as he smoothed the hair away from her flushed face. 'You know where this is going?' His voice was as taut as a bow.

Wasn't she inviting it? God help her, she was practically begging him to make love to her. She took a deep breath, then pushed him away, one hand flat against his chest.

'I'm sorry.'

'Don't be.' He, too, had been unable to diminish the scale of all that he felt for her.

The whole extraordinary episode couldn't have taken more than a few minutes yet she felt she would remember this encounter until the day she died. 'It's all right. I'm all right,' she said. It took a while—she was cautious she wouldn't slip into a faint she was so dazed—but she was able to slide off the cupboard bench, onto the floor. 'I wanted that as much as you,' she said, her voice full of confusion and regret, 'but we have to watch ourselves from now on.'

A week later Carrie was working in a rather desultory fashion on station accounts when her mother rushed into the office, looking violently upset.

Gripped by panic, Carrie sprang to her feet. 'What is it, Mamma?' For a moment she experienced pure dread. Had something happened to her father? Was her mother ill? Had she received some terrible news? Blows had a relentless way of coming right out of the blue.

'It's Scott,' Alicia gasped, sounding quite breathless.

'What's happened? Has he been hurt?' Carrie began to

imagine all sorts of horrendous things. Station accidents were all too common. Even fatalities. She had only seen Scott once since the Sunday of the picnic races. A Scott so repentant, so painfully anxious to please her, she'd found it extremely difficult to say what she needed to say; what desperately needed saying.

Scott, I want out of our engagement!

But the way Scott had acted made her feel breaking their engagement would be too terrible for him to bear at that time. Had she been blinded to the true depth of his love for her? Had she not seen how much he cared? Had she blamed him too severely for that terrible night? She couldn't forget the sight of his hand upraised to her. His excuse was that he was drunk. People acted out of character when they were under the influence of alcohol. Pity for him was part of her self-enforced silence. He had treated her so carefully, as though she were utterly *precious,* and in the end she had let him drive away without saying one word of what was going round and round in her head.

The need for decisive action. It was causing her many a sleepless night. She had the awful feeling once she broke her engagement the recent harmony between herself and her father would break down overnight into icy rejection. Once the thought would have terrified her. But she was a woman now. She was well-educated. She would have to live separate from her parents. That meant she would have to leave her beloved home, the *land* she loved and seek a life for herself in the city. There were far worse things.

Now she led her mother to a chair. 'Mamma, sit down. Here have some water.' Swiftly she poured a glass from the cooler and put it into her mother's hand. 'Scott's been injured, hasn't he?'

'They've *both* been injured,' Alicia said bitterly. Alicia set down the glass of cold water so forcibly it was a wonder it didn't break.

'Both?' Carrie stared at her mother vacantly.

'Scott and that sly, underhanded bitch, Natasha Cunningham,' Alicia said and thrust back a long strand of her hair.

Carrie was stupefied. 'Mamma, what are you talking about? What happened? Where? Why were they together?'

Alicia looked at her daughter with pitying eyes. 'Because he's been seeing her on the side, that's why!'

Carrie couldn't seem to take it in, though she was staring at her mother, hard. 'Scott has been seeing Natasha?' she repeated. Given the way Scott had been behaving towards her—the way he always labelled Natasha 'a bitch'—Carrie found it impossible to believe. Only a few days ago Scott had been literally down on his knees telling her how much he loved her, his voice filled with a I-can't-live-without-you fervour. 'How do you know? Who told you?' Carrie demanded, wondering if there were a possibility her mother had got things wrong.

'The way they found them told the story.' Alicia reached for the glass and drained it as if she were parched to the point of severe dehydration.

'What on earth do you mean?' Carrie's even temper started a slow boil. 'Who found them? Where were they? Spit it out. Mamma, for God's sake! I bet it's all over the district already. Were they in his SUV?'

Alicia clapped her hand to her mouth as though she was about to be sick. 'They careened right off the road and plunged into Campbell's Crossing. It was Ian Campbell who found them. They've already been airlifted to hospital.'

'My God!' Carrie's voice was flat with shock. 'How bad were their injuries?'

'No one knows yet,' Alicia said, forcing herself to steady down. 'Scott was in a worse state than Natasha, I believe.'

Carrie released a devastated groan. 'We must ring the hospital to find out.'

'Carrie, love, did you hear what I told you? Did you take it in? They were *together.* Scott has betrayed you. We all know he and

Natasha were an item one time, but everyone thought it was over. What fools we've all been. Obviously their affair has never left off.'

'I can't understand this,' Carrie said and she couldn't. 'I've been agonising over finding the best moment to tell Scott our engagement is off. I felt desperate to let him down lightly. Now I learn he's been seeing Natasha behind my back all the while. It doesn't make a bit of sense!'

'Doesn't it?' Alicia laughed grimly. 'She was giving him what *you* wouldn't,' she said, bluntly. 'It was just sex.'

'Just sex!' Carrie's voice soared to the ceiling. 'You seem to know a hell of a lot about sex, Mamma.'

Alicia laughed even more bitterly. 'I'm a married woman.' Suddenly tears surged into her eyes. 'Oh, Carrie, what a terrible mess!'

Carrie looked past her mother towards the door. 'I'll have to find out what condition they're both in,' she said. 'I can't stand here wondering. Does Dad know?'

Alicia raised her golden head, looking utterly drained. 'He's the one who told me. He's shocked out of his mind.'

'He never thought to come to me.' Carrie's feeling of wretchedness increased. 'After all, I am supposed to be Scott's fiancée. But Dad came to you. As always.'

'He's dreadfully upset.' Alicia made excuses for her husband. 'Naturally he would come to me, Carrie, and allow me to break the news to you. He was being thoughtful. He's only just got the news directly from Ian Campbell. Your father thought the world of Scott.'

'*You* didn't, Mamma,' Carrie pointed out, without emotion. 'You wouldn't have been too upset if I broke off the engagement.'

Alicia shielded her face with her hand. 'I'm your mother. I wanted to see you marry well. Scott Harper is a great catch. *Was* a great catch.' Her voice broke.

'I pray to God he still will be,' Carrie said, her expression badly strained. 'But not for *me*. Why didn't I recognise what was behind all those snide remarks Natasha used to make? The outright malice in her eyes? I put it down to jealousy. Understandable, when she must have been in love with Scott at one time. Now it appears she's never given up on him. Maybe they were going to continue their affair right into our marriage? I'm a complete fool and I've only just found out. Surely *someone* realised what was going on?'

Alicia lifted her hand, her expression stony. 'They erected a pretty good smoke screen, the two of them,' she said with utter contempt. 'I daresay some of his mates would have known what was going on. They'd think Scotty was entitled to a bit of fun on the side.'

'Fun?' Carrie's voice rose again. 'Fun, for God's sake, *fun*! Well it's not fun now.'

CHAPTER FIVE

HER father was remarkably solicitous. He treated her as if she had been in the accident; as if she were breakable when she didn't feel breakable at all. The town treated her the same way. One would have thought Scott and Natasha had been involved in separate accidents so determined were people not to mention their names in the same breath.

But they *had* been together. There again, no one would tell her what it was about the accident that had so compromised them. Had they been found stark-naked? She rather doubted that. Was Natasha in a state of undress? She finally got it from Paddy when she called into the *Bulletin* office to see him in person—they had spoken on the phone—and ask for time off.

'Needless to say out of respect we won't be printing the full story,' Pat Kennedy told her, studying her face closely. He loved this girl. She was as dear to him as the granddaughter he had wished for but never had.

'At last we get to it,' Carrie sighed, her dark eyes full of misery. 'Tell me, Paddy. Get it over. I guess twenty-four isn't too late to find out you're a gullible fool.'

'You're no fool, my girl,' Paddy said, then added with sudden fierceness, 'it's that fiancé of yours who's the fool. I don't understand this whole business actually. I could have sworn Scott was madly in love with you. No pretence, he couldn't wait to marry you.'

'That's all over, Paddy.'

'He's still in the induced coma?'

Carrie gulped down tears. 'Yes.' Ever one to visualise she had a clear picture of Scott lying in a hospital bed, hooked up to monitors. He had been badly concussed—the great fear being of brain injury—with a broken collarbone, multiple lacerations and two broken ribs. All Carrie wanted was for him to open his eyes again and talk to someone. His mother. She didn't want to be the one but as far as she was concerned all was forgiven. She had no wish for him or Natasha to suffer, though Natasha wasn't the one to worry about right now. Natasha had been lucky. Compared to Scott she had come through relatively unscathed. No broken bones but severe bruising and multiple lacerations that nevertheless were not considered serious enough to leave scars. Carrie was glad of that. Natasha Cunningham was a beautiful woman—if not a beautiful person.

Carrie had spoken to Scott's distraught mother the day of the accident. Thea Harper, after all, was to have become her mother-in-law. All Carrie could do was offer comfort in the face of a mother's agony. Thea was nearly out of her mind with worry, as well she might be. Scott was not only her only son, he was her only child. Both of them had chosen to put Natasha's presence in Scott's SUV to one side. There was enough to worry about without following through on that issue. Time enough for that.

'Are you going to give Scott a chance to tell his side of the story?' Paddy asked, his normally twinkling blue eyes troubled. 'That Cunningham girl is trouble. I've long said so.'

'So what's the full story,' Carrie asked wearily.

Paddy, seasoned journalist, close friend and mentor, with all the wisdom of a fulfilled life, at seventy-three, coloured up. 'It seems Natasha wasn't wearing her, er, shirt. Or her bra,' he added with a shake of his silver head.

Carrie was past shock. 'That seems extraordinarily wild, even for Natasha. Or was it night-time?'

'Must have been,' Paddy said briefly. 'You're going to visit him?'

'Regardless of what they were up to, it's high time I did,' Carrie said. 'I'll look in on Natasha while I'm at it. We've never been friends but I've often thought there's something sad and lost about her. That's why she behaves so badly.'

'Dreadful crowd,' Paddy tutted though he was kind about most people. 'Cruel what they did to Reece and his young family. I've met Clay. He used to be 'little Jimmy Cunningham' back then. I would have met him at the picnic races only for my old mate, Bill Hawkins's funeral in Brisbane. Clay came into the office last week to make himself known to me. I must say he appears to have turned out splendidly.'

Carrie kept her eyes downcast. 'He's a wonderful horse-man. It was quite thrilling to see him win the Cup.'

'Scott must have hated that?' Paddy spoke wryly, showing his understanding of Scott's nature.

'He didn't take it too well,' Carrie agreed. 'Was there some feud in their childhood, Clay and Scott? If so it's carried through to now.'

Paddy's face creased up. 'Scott was a bit of a bully in those days, Carrie,' he settled for, deliberately not mentioning the time Scott Harper had fiercely knocked a younger, smaller child to the ground. 'He chose to pick on Jimmy—I mean Clay—every time he saw him in town. People took sides in those days. Even a child would have been affected. Reece was going to marry Elizabeth Campbell after all. Not that they were engaged. It was just taken for granted. Enter one lovely little English-Irish girl—I never knew which—with blazing Titian hair, and that was that! Elizabeth and Thea Harper were friends. Naturally they turned against Reece and more particularly the young woman he fell in love with.' Paddy's well rounded voice was thin with regret. 'Awful the things that were said about that young woman. Not a single rumour that was sustainable. But mud sticks.'

'I'm wondering how long this particular piece of mud is going to stick?' Carrie sighed. 'I pray for Scott's rapid recovery but I can't marry him, Paddy. I had decided not to even before *this*.'

'Look, who would expect you to?' Paddy asked. He had never thought Golden Boy Harper was half good enough for Carrie.

Carrie stared sightlessly at the wall clock. 'When it happened, Dad was shocked out of his mind. He thought the world of Scott.'

'Yes, isn't that odd?' mused Paddy.

'*You* didn't?' Carrie turned her gaze back on her friend and mentor. He had never said a word against Scott.

Paddy looked embarrassed. 'Well, he's a handsome young fella. He's much admired in certain quarters. He's certainly going to be very rich, but I didn't really see you two as compatible, Carrie. Scott doesn't have your depth of character.'

'Oh, Paddy,' Carrie sighed. 'What depth of character? I'm not much of a judge, am I? Do you think it would be okay if I took this week off? I have to make arrangements to travel to the hospital. What I was going to tell you was, Dad seems to be doubling back on himself. An injured Scott is somehow working his way back to being reinstated in Dad's good books. I can *feel* it! Lately I've been wondering if Dad didn't think my getting myself engaged to Scott was the best thing I've ever done.'

Paddy shook his head. He had to bide his time to speak to Carrie in depth. He had never liked Bruce McNevin any more than he had approved of Scott Harper for Carrie. McNevin, a man of considerable reserve and a dreadful snob, was in Paddy's opinion, a controlling person. In some way he controlled his beautiful, outgoing wife. God knows why! He had long sought to control his daughter as though without his guidance her beauty would cause her to run off the rails. It was all very odd!

Both parents had acted as though the sooner Carrie was married off to a young man they judged right, the better.

Carrie stayed to have a bite of lunch with Paddy and afterwards walked down to the local super market—to stock up on a few items for which her mother had given her a list. It was as she was leaving the huge barn, pushing a laden trolley—why was it one always bought so much more than was on the list?—that she ran in to Clay.

'Hi, I'll take that.'

Her heartbeat stumbled, then staggered on. She watched as he took charge of the trolley. She hadn't spoken to him—neither of them had made contact—since that day on Jimboorie when they had gone into each other's arms. Ecstatic, then, afterwards trying to push away.

'How's Harper?' he asked, following her lead to the parking bay.

'Stable when I rang this morning.'

'And Natasha, my wayward cousin?'

'She'll be coming home. I pray to God they'll both be coming home soon.'

'So how do you feel about it?' he asked, starting to load the provisions into her 4WD.

'I'm just thankful they're alive, Clay. Other than that I feel like a complete fool.'

Clay paused in what he was doing to look down at her. There were faint shadows beneath her beautiful eyes as though she'd slept badly. 'You haven't heard yet what he has to say? I take it at this point you're not *unengaged*?'

'It's a difficult moment to announce the wedding's off,' she countered. 'The town has decided to pretend Natasha's presence in Scott's SUV was quite innocent. She was accompanying him on some journey out to Campbell's Creek a well-known beauty spot for lovers. And at *night*!'

'You don't buy the innocent story?'

She looked away from him, a pressure building up behind her rib cage. 'My mother told me not long after it happened it *wasn't*. She's dreadfully upset. So is my father. Both of them were thrilled when I got engaged to Scott.'

'In God's name, *why*?' There was a lick of anger in his brilliant blue eyes. 'It sounds to me like you were almost railroaded into it.'

She raised a delicate shoulder in a shrug. Let it drop. She realized now there was more than a grain of truth in it. 'Not anymore,' she said. 'When Scott is fit enough I'm going to tell him—'

'For the *second* time—'

'Our engagement is over.' She was wearing a wide-brimmed straw hat, protection against the hot rays of the sun but now a strong gust of wind blew it from her head.

Clay caught it, twirling it in his hand. 'Pretty!' he said, feeling both happy and sad. Something about wide-brimmed straw hats and lovely little faces beneath them made him want to laugh and cry if ever a man was allowed to cry. His mother with a redhead's porcelain complexion, had always worn big shady hats in the sun.

'If he wants to be with Natasha he's welcome to her,' Carrie was saying, sensitive to the changing expressions on his face. *What* was he thinking about?

Clay handed her hat back to her. 'Put it back on. You have the most beautiful skin. I'd say Scott will probably take the line Natasha came onto him. I think that's the sort of thing he would do. The point is, whatever arrangement he had with Natasha, he wants *you*.'

'Maybe for a while.' A little bitterness seeped out. 'But that's not going to happen, Clay.'

'I wish I could believe you,' he smiled ironically.

'What's it to you anyway?' The breathless feeling was increasing. She had never stopped thinking about this man even with everything else going on in her life.

'For a highly intelligent young woman that's a very stupid question,' he said tersely.

She had to breathe in deeply as she looked up at him. His strong features were drawn taut.

'Clay, I'm not taking anything away from…from what happened that day on Jimboorie,' she burst out emotionally. 'I fell…'

'*We* fell…' He corrected, shoving his hands deep in the pockets of his jeans lest he reach out and grab her.

'Are you going to keep interrupting me?' she asked a little raggedly.

'Yes.' He nodded. '*We* fell…'

'Fathoms deep in…*fascination*,' she said, her dark eyes enormous in her face. 'It's not love, Clay. It can't be love. We barely know one another. I've known Scott for most of my life.'

'So?' He pulled at the knotted red bandanna around his bronze throat as though he, too, were having difficulty breathing. 'You got engaged. You pleased your parents, his parents. But he certainly didn't make you happy. Are you going to admit it?'

She looked up at the blazing blue sky—the colour of his eyes—as if looking for an answer. 'I can't abandon him until he's out of hospital and safely home. He could have been killed or condemned to live life in a wheelchair. He could still take a turn for the worse.'

'I hope to God he doesn't,' Clay said, with utter soberness. 'This guy seems to be able to project guilt on you. Are you sorry about *our* time together?' He tilted her chin up. 'Tell me. I'm not here to harass you, Caroline. But I'm not going to stand by and watch you get locked into a bad situation. On your own admission your parents are coming around to dismissing the rumours or ignoring them altogether.'

'Who told *you*?' she asked, curious to know.

'Someone who was there,' he said in a clipped voice.

'Surely not one of the Campbells? You know the story. Your father was supposed to marry Elizabeth Campbell.'

His blue eyes were spangled with silver in the glare. 'Sounds like a lot of railroading goes on in this part of the world. My father told me the only woman he ever wanted to marry was my mother. If you'd have seen them together you would have known how much they loved one another.'

'They both died young,' Carrie lamented.

'Young enough,' Clay said. 'My father never used his name, Cunningham. That's just between you and me. Cunningham was too well-known and he wanted no part of his family anymore. We were the Dysons. Dyson was his second name. We kept ourselves to ourselves. After my father was killed, my mother and I were even more quiet.'

'My heart goes out to you, Clay.' Indeed all of her went out to him.

He could see the sympathy and understanding in her lovely face. 'Don't get upset, Caroline. You know what happened the last time. Do you feel like a cup of coffee?' He was desperate to prolong his time with her.

'I have to get going, Clay,' she made her excuse, seeing station women she knew wheeling out their trolleys and waving to her, eyes curious. She waved back. So did Clay.

'You don't want us to be seen together? Is that it?' His dark-timbred voice turned hard.

'No, I don't mean that.' She shook her head. 'I feel I must visit Scott in hospital. I have to make arrangements. It's a duty I can't avoid.'

He stood there looking down at her, picturing them both back at Jimboorie. 'If you want I can drive you to Toowoomba,' he said. 'Natasha mightn't love me as a cousin should but I've been thinking of calling in to see her. She might need a bit of support. I bet her family are very unhappy with her. Cunninghams *hate* scandals. When would you want to go or did you intend to fly? Are your parents going with you?'

A whole new excitement opened up. Temptation. Danger. 'Not

at this stage. We're all caught in a maze of moral dilemmas, I'm afraid. But I feel I *must* see Scott. I would never forgive myself if anything happened to him. He's been a big part of my life. God, Clay, I was going to marry him in December.'

'Marry *me* instead,' he found himself blurting out when he could well be ruining his chances by speaking out so precipitously. But, hell, wasn't he a better option than Harper?

Carrie's knees nearly gave way from under her. 'You can't be serious?'

His handsome head blocked out the sun. 'I've never been more serious in my life,' he said, flying in the face of caution. 'I wasn't joking when I said I wanted a wife and family. I do. I fully intended to advertise for the right woman. I'd thought it over carefully, came to that decision. Then along came *you*.'

'At what point did you think I might suit?' She feigned a kind of anger.

'Don't get angry,' he said. 'The last thing I intended was offence. Does it matter at what point?' Hadn't he wanted her *instantly*? But to tell her was really to risk frightening her away. 'I think we could make a go of it, Caroline. You'd never feel trapped with me. You love Jimboorie and the old homestead. I've seen that with my own eyes. We could restore it. I'm sure you know all about that side of things.' She was the sort of girl he'd dreamed of but doubted he'd ever find.

Bees were buzzing in a nearby flowering bottle brush or was it a sound in her head? 'Clay, you can't speak to me this way.' She clenched her hands together in agitation.

'Why not?' He lowered his resonant voice lest it float all over the parking area. 'This is a serious proposal. One I'd be honoured if you'd consider. I'm not stone-broke like everyone seems to think. Miracles do happen in life. I've no great fortune, but quite enough to be going on with. I could make a good life for you. I'd dedicate myself to it.'

'You'd marry a woman you didn't love?' She stared up at him, knowing his dedication wouldn't be enough for her. Scales had been lifted from her eyes. She wanted a man who would love her passionately. As passionately as she loved him. Love that would be there to stay.

'You were going to marry a man you didn't love,' he pointed out very quietly.

She felt like she was being swept along in a turbulent stream. 'Clay, I can't possibly consider this. It would take more than I'm prepared to give. Besides, I'm in an impossible place in my life. Haven't you enough admirers already? You could have had your pick of a dozen at the gala dance?'

'What, pretty little teenagers who don't yet know their own minds?'

'There were others!'

'Stop, Caroline,' he said. 'I understand you're in a difficult place. I daresay your parents wouldn't be happy about me, but I know we can make a real go of it. I can't put it better than that. Except to say I'm as strongly attracted to you as you are to me. Okay, it's not love. You say you can't fall in love right away. But what we have is *good*.'

She couldn't deny it. What they had was beautiful. No one could take that kiss away, but exposing her heart with all that had happened to her seemed an ominous thing to do. Her fellow shoppers would probably think she was flirting with Clay when Scott was lying comatose in a hospital bed.

Knowing what sort of person Carrie was, the other women shoppers *weren't* thinking that at all, but Carrie found herself burdened by unwarranted guilt.

'When are you wanting to leave?' Clay asked, oblivious of anyone now but Carrie.

'Tomorrow morning,' she said. 'It would be a three-hour drive even moving!'

'I'll take you,' he said.

'So how would we meet up?' she asked shakily. God, she wanted so much to be with him when she didn't even know if she could handle it. Her whole philosophy of life was coming under bombardment. It was as though a volcano lying dormant within her was showing perilous signs of erupting.

'What the hell, I'll drive out to Victory Downs,' Clay decided. 'I'll get an early start. What have we got to hide anyway? I'm going to see my cousin. You're going to see your ex-fiancé. No need for me to come in and meet the folks,' he said with extreme dryness. 'You can come out to the car.'

Carrie shook her head. She just couldn't face her father's opposition. It would be like a great icy wind from Antarctica. 'I'll meet you in town. I'll park here.'

'What time can you make it?' He didn't like the idea of her making all these long drives.

'Eight o'clock. Is that too late?'

'Eight's fine. Put in a few clothes. You'll be tired. We might as well stay in Toowoomba overnight.' His blue eyes looked directly into hers. 'Trust me, Caroline. We'll be fine.'

Did she trust him?

That wasn't the question at all. The answer was and it came right away. Did she trust *herself?*

When she found Scott's room, his parents were already there, seated at their son's bedside.

'Carrie, dear!' Thea Harper rose at once, coming to hug and kiss her. 'I'm so glad you're here.'

'Carrie!' Even Bradley Harper's severe face broke into a smile. 'Thanks for coming. How did you get here?'

'Drove,' Carrie said, cutting off the conversation by moving quickly towards the bed. 'How is he?' She bent over Scott's prone frame, gently, even tenderly, taking his hand. 'Any change?'

'They've wound down the drugs,' Thea Harper said, in a shaky voice. 'They're waiting for him to come out of it.'

Carrie lowered herself into the chair Bradley Harper drew up for her close to Scott's head. He looked very young and handsome. Sleeping quietly except for the monitors. 'He's going to be all right,' she said.

'Oh, God, he has to be!' Thea Harper suddenly started to sob.

'Thea, stop that,' her husband commanded. 'You're wearing yourself out. Scotty's going to be okay now Carrie's here.'

Please, please, please, don't put this on me, Carrie thought, something like panic crawling across her skin.

How was she supposed to feel when Scott had been continuing an affair with his old flame? Ready to forgive and forget? It seemed so. As far as the Harpers were concerned she and Scott were destined for marriage no matter what! The Harpers adored their only child so much they were prepared to make any sacrifice for him including *her*. If, God forbid, Scott were to be confined to a wheelchair they would still expect her to go through with the marriage. If she loved him, she would. Now she fully understood she didn't love him.

The Harpers, sick and exhausted, had gone off to have coffee leaving Carrie still sitting by Scott's bed. She, too, had shut her eyes as a headache pressed down on her temples, although she was still gently holding his fingers.

'Carrie?'

Her eyes flew open. She hadn't imagined that. Scott had spoken, sounding perfectly lucid. 'You're awake. Oh, thank God!'

'What happened?'

His dilated pupils seemed impossibly large. 'It's okay. You're all right,' she patted him reassuringly. 'You're in hospital. You were in an accident. You were badly concussed. Hang on, I have to get a doctor in here.' She rose from her chair.

'Don't leave me,' Scott called. 'Don't ever leave me.'

Carrie flew out to the nurses' station, her mind swirling with crazy thoughts of flight.

The Harpers were ecstatic. 'It was *you*!' Thea Harper, laughing and crying gave Carrie all the credit. 'He heard your voice. He felt the touch of your hand.'

'He was ready to come out of it, Mrs. Harper,' Carrie said, aware Scott's doctor was studying her with a close but friendly eye.

'No, *you* were the miracle!' Thea maintained, hugging Carrie yet again, her exhaustion lifted. 'You, Carrie McNevin. You're an angel.'

An angel, imagine!

'Look I'll have to shoo you all out for ten minutes or so,' the doctor said. 'You can come back one at a time and say your goodbyes. This sleeping beauty might have awakened, but he's still in need of plenty of rest.'

'We'll go,' Bradley Harper said, putting an arm around his wife. 'Love you, son!' A hard, tough man, he declared it in a strong, emotional voice. That hurt Carrie. She doubted her father could ever say that to *her*. Certainly not in that voice. 'We'll be back later,' Brad Harper said.

'Don't go, Carrie,' Scott appealed to Carrie, his eyes glassy. 'I need you here. Carrie?'

She looked at the doctor unsure what to do. 'She can come back later,' the doctor said. 'Settle back, young man. You want to get out of here as soon as possible, don't you?'

'Can't wait. Everything is going to be okay, Carrie,' Scott said and it seemed to her there was full comprehension in his eyes. 'Kiss me before you go.'

She bent over him, touching her lips to his temple. 'I'll come back later, okay?'

'I love you,' Scott said, as though there were no other woman in the world.

* * *

The Harpers were waiting for her down the corridor. Thea reached out to hug her yet again. 'You're really a godsend, Carrie. *You* are the one he needs.'

The pressure was getting scary. 'We should talk about that, Mrs. Harper, but not today,' Carrie said. 'Are you going to look in on Natasha? She hasn't been discharged yet.'

'Of course we're not going to look in on that scheming young woman,' Thea said. 'She's done nothing but throw herself shamelessly at Scott.'

'It appears I was the only one who didn't know that,' Carrie said quietly.

'My son loves only *you*, Carrie,' Brad Harper told her in a voice that defied her to disagree. 'Natasha Cunningham meant nothing to him.'

'Actually she did, Mr. Harper,' Carrie said, inside objecting to his domineering tone. Why did men want so much power over women? 'But let's not spoil the moment. Scott is going to make a full recovery.'

'Thank God!' the Harpers declared in unison. 'Come and have a coffee with us, Carrie,' Thea invited. 'We're drowning in it but we can have tea.'

'Thank you, Mrs. Harper, but I intend to look in on Natasha,' Carrie said, letting them make what they liked of that.

'Good! Give her what for!' Brad Harper advised, his weathered face grim.

Natasha Cunningham was not in bed. She was sitting in an armchair looking out the window, her back to Carrie. No one else was in the room. Clay must have gone, although they had made arrangements to meet up late afternoon.

'Natasha, it's me, Carrie,' she said in as gentle a voice as she could muster.

A moment of stunned silence, then, 'What the hell are *you*

doing here?' Natasha responded roughly. She thrust up and turned around as if prepared for confrontation.

'I would have thought that obvious,' Carrie said. 'I came to see how you are. Knowing what your family is like I thought you could do with a friend.'

'Ain't that the truth!' Natasha was half laughing now, but she looked terrible. She was white and drained, her eyes bloodshot and red rimmed as though she had never stopped crying. The right side of her face was black and blue all around the jawline. Lacerations were clearly visible on her lower neck and arms. She wasn't in hospital garb. She was wearing a T-shirt and loose linen trousers that hung on her. Always bone thin, she had lost even more weight.

'Thank God you got out of it as well as you did,' Carrie said. 'Please sit down again. You don't look so good.'

'How's Scotty?' Natasha asked, leaning over as though her stomach ached. 'I dared not go near his room.'

'I was about to tell you. *When* you sit down. Preferably lie down.'

'Okay, okay.' Natasha waved a hand irritably, but she went back to the bed. 'How is he?' She stared Carrie right in the eye.

'You know he's been in a medically induced coma. He's fully conscious now. He recognises everyone. The fractured clavicle will keep him quiet for a couple of months and he can forget polo for a while longer, but he'll heal. His doctor is expecting him to make a full recovery. His youth and fitness will be a big help.'

There was an unbearably intense look or gladness and relief on Natasha's face. Then she burst into violent tears. 'It was all my fault. Everything is my fault.'

Carrie could only feel pity. 'Are you well enough to talk about it or should we let it go?' Her very nature was preventing her from feeling the ill will towards Natasha she thoroughly deserved.

'You must be furious with me. Furious and disgusted.'

Natasha dashed her tears away with the back of her head. 'I'm a bitch. A real bad bitch. I've gloried in it.'

'No, you haven't.' Carrie shook her head, suddenly convinced it was true. 'Somehow I think you've been pushed into that role. I'm not furious with you. I don't exactly understand why. By rights, I should be.' Carrie reached inside her handbag for some clean tissues, which she passed to Natasha. 'Did you have an argument? Was that it? Scott lost control of the wheel?' She could well see it happening. Natasha was such a volatile young woman.

'Do you love him, Carrie?' Natasha didn't answer Carrie's questions but asked one of her own. 'He's a real bastard you know.'

'But *you* love him,' Carrie pointed out, doing her own ignoring.

'God knows why! I've always loved him. I've tried, but I could never get myself free of him. He took *my* virginity, you know. I might have held on to it longer if not for him. And he wasn't too gentle about it, either. Scotty only thinks about *himself.*'

'It certainly looks like it,' Carrie agreed. 'And you've been with him all this time?'

Natasha wept afresh, charcoal smudges beneath her eyes. 'He's as mad as he can be for you, but you wouldn't come across. He told me. I could barely stop laughing. I, unlike you, couldn't keep away from him. Not that he ever turned me down. Sex is very high on Scotty's agenda.'

'A little bit *too* high, if you ask me,' Carrie said, crisply.

Natasha nodded as though they were two friends having a serious discussion. 'He even wanted it the night of the dance when he had that fight with Clay.'

'Oh my Lord!' Carrie groaned softly. 'And that's the man I got myself engaged to! How utterly blind I've been.'

'Don't sound so shocked.' Natasha picked up a few white grapes and popped them in her mouth. 'He needed comfort. He knows I can give it to him. None of this little bit of loving stuff like you dish out.'

'Thanks for sharing that with me, Natasha,' Carrie said. 'You're one underhanded pair and it's starting to show.'

Natasha laughed. 'You're a very dull person, Carrie. Face it. I have more than a few tricks.'

'Of course you have,' Carrie said. 'Even then Scott isn't all that interested in you.'

'*You* don't love him,' Natasha cried, mortally stung.

'You'd have been ready to do violence had I truly taken your man.'

'You bet!' Natasha wiped her mouth with the back of her hand. 'I'd have skinned you alive.'

'Only I wouldn't stoop to prostituting myself with another woman's fiancée,' Carrie said flatly. 'Has Clay been to see you?'

She didn't expect to see a smile break across Natasha's face. 'You know my cousin's a really nice guy when you get to know him. One of the *good* guys. I didn't get to know too many of them. Scott got in the way. Clay would never tell a woman to get herself an abortion.'

Carrie felt like an avalanche had hit her. *Abortion!* She could even feel herself turn pale.

'I'm sorry, Carrie,' Natasha burst out. 'I'm really and truly sorry. You're a good guy, too. You've always been nice to me even when I've been a pig.'

Carrie hardly heard her. 'You're pregnant?' she asked, astonished now Natasha hadn't caused it to happen long before this.

Natasha's answer came right away, not without a trace of triumph. 'I am.'

'Even through the accident?' It was a mystery to Carrie.

'Strong little beggar,' Natasha said, fondly.

'How far along are you?'

'Ten weeks,' Natasha said, patting her flat tummy.

'Did you tell Clay?'

'God no!' Natasha looked astounded by the question. 'Of

course I didn't. What's it got to do with him? Strewth, he was acting like *you're* the love of his life. What's with you anyway that the guys get so carried away?'

'*You're* the one who got carried away, Natasha,' Carrie said, her expression firming. 'Either that or you decided to resolve the situation. I wouldn't put it past you.'

'It wasn't like that,' Natasha said.

Carrie shook her head. 'You have a gnat's sense of what's right and wrong, Natasha. And Scott suggested you get an abortion?'

'Not suggested, dear. Scott's not like that. It was a command. It's *you* he wants to marry. I'm beginning to wonder if you little virgins aren't the smartest of us all.'

Carrie ignored the comment; instead she asked, 'What are you going to do about the baby?'

Natasha touched her stomach tenderly again. 'I don't know yet. This will be a great, great scandal unless I pack up and leave home in a hurry.'

'Do your parents know?'

Natasha shook her dark head vehemently. 'Come off it, Carrie. We're talking the world's most sanctimonious people. It's just you, me and Scotty. And the doctor who examined me, of course and he's not talking.'

'You must keep the baby, Natasha,' Carrie said, trying hard to deal with all this. 'It's precious new life you're carrying. This is *your* child. You'll regret it all the days of your life if you allow yourself to be talked into an abortion. Your little one has put up a fight for life so far.'

'That he has. It's a boy, I know. Scotty's son.' Natasha stretched out a leisurely hand for more grapes, her expression showing maternal pride.

Carrie's head was swimming so badly she might have been drunk. There was an ache in her heart. A worse ache in her head.

'So you'd better get Scotty to marry you,' she said, somehow finding the strength to stand up. 'I wouldn't touch him with a barge pole.'

CHAPTER SIX

THEY sat in a quiet corner of a little restaurant at the top of the Range, a twinkling world of coloured lights spread out across the city beneath them.

'No appetite?' Clay asked, having watched her toy with the delicious food.

'I should have stuck with the entrée,' Carrie said, putting down her knife and fork. 'The food's great, but life's getting too much for me.' Her dark velvety eyes registered sadness.

'Scott's going to make a full recovery,' he pointed out. 'That must take a lot of the burden off you.' He hoped to God it did. Maybe then she could tell Scott to let go.

'It does,' she admitted.

'Is there something you're not telling me?'

'Yes.' He was just so perceptive, she dipped her head.

'Thought so.' He let his eyes rest on her. She was wearing a bare little black top with a multi-coloured, multi-patterned gauzy skirt that almost reached her ankles. Her beautiful long hair braided away from her face shone pure gold in the candlelight. Her skin had an equally lovely gold tint. He had never seen any woman he thought more beautiful. No woman to touch her.

'Obviously it's very much upset you?' He topped up her glass of white wine.

'Thank you.' She raised her glass and took a long sip. 'This is in complete confidence, because I trust you.'

Warning bells began ringing inside his head. 'Just so long as you're not about to tell me you're going to marry Harper in December?' His eyes sizzled over her.

'I'm *not* going to marry Scott,' she said and shook her head. 'Chances are when he's fit enough—or even before then—he'll be marrying Natasha.'

Clay sat back, astonished, though Carrie had delivered the news quite matter-of-factly. 'Now that's the very *last* thing I expected to hear.'

'She's pregnant,' Carrie explained, still in that quiet even tone. 'I had to tell someone. I couldn't keep it to myself. Natasha is pregnant with my ex-fiancé's child.'

'God!' Clay was genuinely stunned. 'Doesn't she know about contraception?'

Finally Carrie released a long-baffled sigh. 'Being Natasha I'd say she took her chances. She could even have been trying to push her luck. Who knows? The fact is, she's carrying Scott's child.'

'Then he must marry her,' Clay said as though there were no other course open to the man.

'He told her to have an abortion.'

Clay couldn't disguise his contempt. 'Doesn't that say everything you need to know about Scott Harper? His *own* child and he's ready to destroy it? Natasha can't listen to him. Times have changed so much. She'll get through and she'll adore her baby.'

'I hope so,' Carrie said, thinking the essence of the Cunninghams was their coldheartedness. 'There aren't too many families like yours.'

'They're not *my* family,' Clay retorted, his voice peppered with loathing. 'Nor will they ever be in my mind. I gather Natasha doesn't get along too well with her parents. It doesn't make sense to me, these rich people. They have everything and they have nothing. Then again Natasha is getting looked after so well financially she'd never leave home.'

Carrie drank her wine slowly. 'I would say that's because of Scott.' Natasha wasn't far off thirty and on her own admission she hadn't really looked beyond her first lover.

'The bastard!' Clay exploded, then apologised.

'No need, you're spot on. Scott has always been in the picture.'

'Poor Natasha!' Clay said. 'Though she doesn't seem to have much going for her in the way of morals. But she was nice for the time I was with her. Quiet and introspective. Now I know why. In a way it's the same for her as you. Harper caught both of you into a trap.'

Carrie tasted the bitter truth. 'I'm thinking Natasha turned the tables on him.'

'You said it's over?' Clay caught the tips of her fingers across the table.

'It's over,' she said, reacting to the thrill of his hand on hers.

'But you haven't told him?'

She averted her dark eyes. 'When he's settled back at home Scott and I will be having a serious talk.'

'I'm really happy to hear that,' Clay said, not looking happy at all. 'He surely doesn't think Natasha is going to do as he says?'

'He'd have to be forced to marry her,' Carrie gave her opinion. 'I don't think his parents would force him to do anything. Especially after his accident which apparently Natasha caused.'

'I'm sure she didn't plan it. I guess he went ballistic when she told him.'

'I would say his reaction would be fairly strong.'

'Anyway, that's their problem. Natasha's child is the Harper's grandchild. Surely that means everything to them? Their *grandchild*? The Cunninghams aren't nobodies. Natasha's parents would adjust overnight. So would the town if Scott and Natasha were to marry.'

'Nothing would surprise me,' Carrie said, 'but I have the awful feeling some of the scandal will stick to *me.*'

'You're the innocent party,' Clay said.

'That won't stop it. It never does. I don't feel like I'm walking on solid ground any more.'

'I can understand that,' he said quietly. 'You're in shock. You have to give yourself a little time, Caroline.'

'*You* have to give me a little time.' She looked into his eyes, sealing the rest of the world off.

'I'd give you all the time in the world if only we had it,' he replied. 'I know what's in my head already.' He could, and perhaps should, have said what's in 'my head and my *heart.*' It was true enough, but she still wasn't absolutely free of Harper. 'I know it came out all wrong the last time. I startled you. I see now I could hardly fail to do so, but I'm here for you, Caroline, once Harper is out of the way. I seem to have been alone for so much of my life. It wasn't only my father who left me. My mother left me as well after he was killed. Neither of them returned.'

She pressed her hands against the heat in her cheeks. It flamed through her whole body. 'What if you found you couldn't love me? *After* marriage, for all your best intentions it just didn't happen?' It was a legitimate fear.

All Clay wanted to do was rain kisses on her face, her throat, her breasts, down over her whole body to her toes as beautifully formed as were her slender fingers. Fingers that were doubly pretty because she wasn't wearing Harper's ring. When had she taken that off?

'I refuse to believe it couldn't happen,' he said. 'Didn't a fire burn inside you when I kissed you?'

She was almost ready to tell him his kiss had awakened her to full life only she held back. 'This is the wrong time for a courtship, Clay,' she said. 'You know it's funny, but sometimes, I badly want to call you James,' she confessed.

'So you can call me James when we marry.' He gave her the smile that so easily melted her heart.

'I think it's time to take me back to the hotel,' she murmured, just that little bit scared of so much emotion. When she was with Clay she wasn't prim and proper Carrie. She was someone else.

'Do you intend seeing Harper again in the morning before we return?' he asked, somehow sensing what was actually in her mind. He, too, was overwhelmed by the powerful attraction that had overtaken them. He had wished for the right woman. It had happened. But he could see she was so unguarded she could snap.

'I don't want to, but I will.' Carrie spoke more firmly. 'Hospitals aren't the best places to deliver bad news. And it *will* be bad news for Scott and his parents. Scott has lived his life thinking he can have any girl he wants. For whatever his reasons he's hell-bent on marrying me. Perhaps it was because I wasn't giving him what he wanted? I had to be absolutely *his* and marriage was the only way? Who knows? He was only using Natasha when she lay in bed with him. I feel sorry for her. Nevertheless at this point he's too sick to tell him what I think of him. That will have to wait.'

'So we're going around in circles?' Clay realized he had to accept that. He gestured to the waiter for the bill.

'It's a bit like that.' Briefly Carrie met his gaze.

She was standing quietly in the foyer, admiring the exquisite flower arrangement—this after all was the Garden City of Queensland—while Clay settled the bill.

He joined her after a moment and took her arm. They were barely out the door when they were confronted by a well dressed middle-aged couple about to enter the restaurant. It was the Harpers, even though Carrie had been given to understand that Bradley Harper was returning home, leaving his wife staying with a friend who lived on the Range.

Carrie felt so guilty she might have been caught in the execution of a serious crime.

The Harpers, too, looked startled.

'What on earth are you doing here, Carrie? And with *him*?' Shock quickly turned to outright aggression as Bradley Harper addressed her in his deep, gravelly voice. He snapped a furious glance over Clay who stood, a tall, quiet presence by Carrie's side.

'Good evening, Mr and Mrs Harper,' Carrie said in her usual courteous manner. 'You remember Clay, don't you? Clay Cunningham?'

'Yes,' Thea Harper said briefly, incapable of arranging her face into a smile. She was pale with dismay. 'What are you doing here together, Carrie? I don't understand. Scott's still lying in hospital and you've had dinner with this young man? I really can't believe it. Not *you*, Carrie. You always conduct yourself so well.'

'I hope I'm still doing that, Mrs. Harper,' Carrie said. 'Clay is my friend. Nothing more.' That wasn't true but they didn't have to know. 'Many things have changed since before and after Scott's accident. I'm so glad he's going to make a full recovery but Scott knows in his heart our engagement is over. It just wasn't the right time to make that perfectly plain to him at the hospital. I'll delay our talk until he's well enough.'

The Harpers stood staring at her. 'You're not *serious*? You can't be, Carrie,' Thea Harper moved forward to lay a hand on Carrie's arm. 'You're overreacting surely? My son adores you.'

'That's not true, Mrs. Harper,' Carrie said very gently. 'I don't want to distress you. I know how upset you and Mr. Harper have been, but Scott really is involved with Natasha. I'll allow him to tell you about it himself.'

Bradley Harper broke in so violently he must have reached breaking point. 'Involved with Natasha Cunningham, rubbish! There are always women like Natasha Cunningham in life. What

I want to know is, what's been going on between *you* two?' His expression turned ugly.

Clay spoke for the first time. 'Have a care, Mr. Harper,' he said in a very quiet, controlled sort of voice.

'What was that? Speak up?' Bradley Harper, a powerful man, began to square up, looking at the six-foot-three, superbly fit young man as though he were an insect to be crushed underfoot.

'You heard me perfectly well the first time,' Clay said. 'We're in public, remember? I suggest you back down. And you might apologise to Caroline. She's the injured party here.'

'*Caroline?*' Harper's expression froze. 'She's not *Caroline*. She's Carrie. Don't get smart with me, son!' Bradley Harper warned, his beefy, still handsome face flushed with blood. 'I saw off your father. I'll do the same for you.'

'I wouldn't bank on that.' Clay's alert stance and sombre tone would have convinced anyone. 'As I understand it you didn't see off my father, as you call it. Your men saw him off your station at gunpoint. You didn't appear at all. I'm not like my father anyway. My father was a *gentle* man. I'm not.'

A rush of contemptuous laughter broke from Bradley Harper's mouth. 'Why you arrogant young bastard!' That peculiar smile broadened as he threw a rage packed right hook, which Clay blocked so effectively the older man went staggering back. Like father. Like son.

Both women were utterly dismayed. 'Please. Please stop it!' Carrie begged. This wasn't what they wanted. Other people were coming out of the restaurant, staring at them, whispering.

'You'll be sorry for that!' Bradley Harper snarled at Clay after he righted himself and regained a little control. 'How dare you lay a hand on me? Do you even have a clue how powerful I am?'

'You're not above the law, Mr Harper,' Clay reminded him, in a voice that held a natural authority. 'What you attempted was assault. *I'll* lay charges if you ever attempt anything like that again. Believe me, I only stopped you because of the ladies and the fact I knew you'd come off badly.'

The tears were spilling down Thea Harper's face. 'Brad, please! You're making a spectacle of us.' She'd had the feeling all along it wasn't a good idea for Brad to bring her here. Now *this*!

'*These two* are making the show,' Bradley Harper corrected her with surprising venom.

'I'm sorry, Mrs Harper.' Carrie, who was trembling badly, took Clay's arm to move him away. She could feel the tension right through his body—the desire she supposed, to pummel Bradley Harper as he had pummelled Scott. There were old issues that had to be settled here, though she knew it wouldn't be Clay who would make the first move. He'd simply finish it.

Neither of them said a word all the way back to the hotel where they were staying.

'I feel like a drink,' Clay said softly, when they entered the hotel lobby. 'Care to join me?'

'I'll sit for a while,' she said, too upset to go up to her room. 'I feel very shaky. He's an awful man, Brad Harper.'

'Of course he is.' Clay led her into the well-appointed lounge where a few guests were seated at the small circular tables. 'You can count your lucky stars you won't be getting him for a father-in-law after all.'

'Mrs Harper is okay.' She sank into a plush banquette, resting her back against it. 'She's easy enough to get on with, but she's right under his thumb, poor woman. He's such a domineering man. Even Scott is intimidated by his father.'

'Bag of wind,' Clay said, dismissing the powerful and ruthless Bradley Harper. 'What can I get you?'

'I don't especially want anything.' Yes, she did. She wanted his arms around her.

'What about a brandy and ginger? You want something to settle you down. I'm for a single malt whiskey. Don't move from this spot. I'll be back in a moment.'

Her mother and father would soon get the news, Carrie thought, watching Clay walk over to the bar. When he arrived there, he turned and looked back at her. Even at a distance his eyes *burned* an electric-blue.

She gave him a little wave, conscious women at other tables were looking at him as well. And why not? He was a marvellous looking man. She hadn't planned on falling in love with him. Yet here she was with him. She saw him give the order to the bartender, then he returned to the table, settling his tall, rangy frame into the banquette beside her.

Carrie drew great comfort from his nearness. Comfort and a kind of bliss that flushed her skin and made her look as though she were lit from within.

'What's with the Harpers always throwing punches?' he asked, wryly. 'Wild punches, I might add.'

'They see themselves as men of action,' Carrie said, with a crazy impulse to lay her head on his shoulder.

'Better to think first and act later,' Clay said, looking towards the waiter who was approaching with their drinks.

Carrie took not a sip, but a gulp of her drink. Things were getting right out of hand. The encounter with the Harpers had really thrown her. Her drink was cold and the shot of brandy added depth to the sparkling ginger ale. 'Mrs Harper won't lose any time ringing my parents to let them know they've seen me with you,' she said, one part of her admiring the paintings around the walls. 'They'll do it tonight.'

'It's always best to say exactly what you're doing, Caroline,' he told her quietly. 'You're a grown woman not a child. You could have told your mother I was giving you a lift.'

'I did,' she said.

'Well, that's not so bad then?' He studied her pure profile. 'Would she tell your father?'

Carrie shook her head. 'No. I'm beginning to think there's lots my mother doesn't tell my father. Sometimes I can't figure Mamma out. She does things I know she doesn't want to, to please Dad.'

'Lots of wives would do that.'

'Mamma does it for a *living*,' Carrie said. 'It's all coming to a head, isn't it?'

'It has to, Caroline. You have to get on with your life. Whether I'm in it or not remains to be seen.'

'Sure you don't want to run that advertisement?' she asked, tilting her head to stare into his eyes.

'Only if you write it up for me.'

'Let's see, how would it go?'

'You're the journalist,' he reminded her.

'Photojournalist,' she corrected with a little smile. 'I take photos for the *Bulletin* as well.'

'I'm certain you'll take a good one of me. Now where were we?'

'Bush Bachelor, twenty-eight, never married, very fit, owns his own pastoral property, is looking for a wife aged between—?'

'Twenty-four and twenty-eight,' he filled in, in a helpful tone of voice. 'Under twenty-four too young to really know their own mind, over twenty-eight older than me. Twenty-four for preference. Petite. Must be a golden-blonde with velvety-brown doe eyes. A countrywoman, loves the land, an excellent horse-woman, interested in restoring a historic homestead, eventually having kids, two or three, must be able to guarantee a daughter who looks just like her. Let's see, what else?'

'You don't need me at all,' she said. She took another little swallow. Even tried a smile.

'Oh, yes, I do. Haven't I just described you?'

'Maybe I was the first one your gaze really fell on?' she suggested. 'Maybe knowing I was Scott Harper's fiancée had something to do with it?'

'What is that supposed to mean, Caroline?'

The question was dead serious. 'Didn't Brad Harper fire up when you called me Caroline?' she remarked, ignoring his question. 'You'd think that wasn't allowed.'

'Answer the question, please.' He gently tapped the back of her hand.

'Maybe you felt like taking something of his?'

He kept looking at her until she looked away. 'Actually I'm fine with that, but the thought never crossed my mind. I saw the connection as a huge complication. I definitely wanted to get to know you better, but there you were, engaged.'

The air around them seemed on the point of igniting. 'I'm sorry,' Carrie apologised.

'So you should be. But I'll forgive you. This one time.'

'It could just as easily have been someone else. One of the McFadden sisters,' she persisted. 'Jade or Mia. Both of them are very attractive and good company. They're station people. They're good riders. Jade and I often battle it out for first place in competitions. They certainly gave the impression they were attracted to you.'

'So we've narrowed it down to the McFadden sisters and *you*.'

Inside she was deeply, *deeply*, shaken. 'I can't see clearly about myself, Clay. You've got to heed it. What I do see is a twenty-four-year-old woman who was about to marry a man who continued to sleep with other women—I bet there were others—while we were engaged, then he impregnated one. Finally to cap it off a man who told another woman to get rid of his own child so he could still marry me. What kind of a fool did he think I was? What kind of a fool am I for that matter?'

'What kind of a callous bastard is he, don't you mean?' Clay responded, with frightening calm. 'Countless people have been deceived, Caroline. Men and women. They give their trust only to have it trampled underfoot. One doesn't have to be a fool for that to happen. It happens right across the board.'

'Trust is so very important,' she said quietly. 'It is to me yet it's so easy to lose faith. What happens then? Does one turn into a cynic, never trusting anyone again?'

'You know what they say! Life's a gamble. Love's a gamble. We come through with courage and a dollop of daring.'

'And there's another thing about me,' she said. 'I don't know my own mind. I'd be devastated if I'd truly loved Scott. Obviously I didn't. I just thought I was in love with him.'

'So when did you wake up to the fact you weren't?' he asked dryly. 'Did it just happen one morning?'

She turned her head slightly. 'The fact I could so easily be attracted to you was a tremendous eye opener. What if it had happened *after* I married Scott?'

'No need to worry about it,' he consoled her. 'You're not going to marry Scott. We might leave the rest of that drink.'

'Are you saying I've had too much?' There was a little flash in her dark eyes.

'Perhaps the tiniest little bit. You had very little to eat and that confrontation with the Harpers upset you.'

'Didn't it upset you?'

'I wanted to hit that man,' Clay admitted, his handsome face taut. 'I wanted to hit him so badly, but he's too old to hit. And then there were you women. Women don't like violence.'

'You're right about that!' she wholeheartedly agreed. 'I'm apprehensive about what my father is going to say.'

'He's very tough on you in his way, isn't he? Why *is* that?' He studied her, a beautiful, refined young woman any father would be proud of. He was quite unable to understand it.

Carrie suddenly picked up her glass and clinked it against his in a funny little gesture. 'Our personalities are incompatible?' she suggested, with a brittle little laugh. 'There's something about me he doesn't like? I suppose it can happen.'

'Leave home, Caroline,' he advised. 'It's time you did.'

'Victory Downs isn't going to be mine, anyway,' she sighed. She didn't want the rest of her drink but she had it anyway.

'How's that?' A vertical line appeared between his strongly marked brows. 'You're an only child. Who else can take over?'

'My cousin, Alex, will inherit. He's still a student.'

'Good God!' Clay found himself appalled. 'So what's your little lot?'

'Did you think I was an heiress?' she asked, outright challenge glimmering in her eyes. 'Did you think you just could land an heiress? You didn't put that in the ad.'

'Caroline, I couldn't care less if you were penniless,' he said a little curtly. 'It's *you,* the woman, I'm interested in.'

'That's what they all say.' He was quite right. She was just that tiny bit intoxicated. 'I'll be "well looked after" I've been told. Besides, I was to marry Bradley Harper's heir. That was considered a compelling reason for matrimony.'

'How very mercenary,' he said with contempt.

'Only I'm not marrying anyone,' she said.

They took the lift to Carrie's floor walking down the quiet, empty corridor to her room. There they paused while Carrie hunted up her keycard.

'You seem to be taking an awfully long time,' he said, an attractive wry note in his voice.

'Damn, where is it?' She knew she had it. 'I know!' She sank her hand into the deep hidden pocket in her skirt.

'Here, give it to me.' He took the keycard from her, opening up the door. 'Good night, Caroline,' he said.

'Goodness, you sound as if you have a very pressing engagement elsewhere. Are you that anxious to get rid of me!' She pushed past him and entered the comfortably furnished room, switching on more lights. Am I about to make a fool of myself? she thought. Why not? He already knows I am.

'Come here,' he said gently, standing just inside the door.

She spun about. 'There's nothing going to happen, Clay.'

'What makes you suppose there was?' His blue eyes gave off sparks.

'The way you're looking at me for one thing,' she said, trying to keep her emotional equilibrium and losing the battle. 'I'm a virgin. Did I mention that? It's a joke these days.'

He stayed where he was. He wasn't smiling. 'Why wouldn't a woman keep herself for the man she truly loves?'

'For fear she mightn't find him and life is flying by. I'm sorry, Clay. I'm trying to tell you I'm not a good judge.'

'You're tired,' he said. 'Exhausted.'

'We both are. Do you want to sleep with me in this bed?'

He didn't say anything for a moment. He just wanted to look at her. 'I don't think I'd be doing much sleeping,' he said, finally. 'I told you, Caroline. There's no pressure.'

'That's something else!' she said raggedly, doing a half spin. 'Scott was ready to wait. Next thing he's trying to rape me.'

Clay remembered that night very clearly; the way he had felt. 'Don't remind me! That would never happen to *any* woman with me, Caroline. You know that. Come on now, you're tired and upset. You'll get over all this. It's been pretty full on, one thing after another.'

'And another to face,' she said, leaning wearily against an armchair.

'I'm driving you back to Victory Downs tomorrow,' he told her firmly. 'We can get your 4WD picked up from the town and delivered to the station. I don't want you pushing on home.'

She wasn't looking forward to it, either. 'There'd be fireworks, Clay,' she warned.

He wasn't worried for himself. 'Your father's temper wouldn't bother me any more than Brad Harper's. I didn't think your father gave way to emotion anyway, he looks so darn buttoned up.'

For a moment Carrie looked quite lost. 'I should have said iceworks, not fireworks. Dad freezes you out.'

'I'm driving you home, Carrie,' Clay repeated. 'Right to your door. Now come here.'

Adrenaline shot into her bloodstream. All her senses lifted and began to soar. 'What for?'

'I want to kiss you,' he said simply, not taking his eyes off her. 'I want to take your *kiss* with me to bed.'

What else could she do? Every cell in her body demanded it. She walked towards him as if she couldn't keep away.

His arms were around her, his hand at the back of her neck, taking the weight off her head. He was so much taller he was lifting her, enveloping her. He bore her weight so easily her feet were clear of the ground.

'Caroline!' he breathed, over her head.

Then his marvellous mouth came down on hers. She was so hungry, *greedy* to keep it there. What had happened to that *absent* part of her? The part Scott had never been able to reach? Did she only come alive through this man? The pleasure he gave her was so sensual, so limb melting, she thought as she collapsed against him. At any rate she relaxed into a posture of utter submission waiting for him to open her up like a flower.

All her defences were tumbling. She gathered nectar from his open mouth, kissing and nibbling at those cleanly defined, upraised edges as she went.

They were breathing as one.

It was an agony and an ecstasy to kiss and be kissed like this. The one counter-balancing the other. Agony. Ecstasy. But she wanted more. Much more. She realised now she was desperately in need of love. She wanted *everything* a man and a woman in love did together. It was impossible to resist longing such as this. Such was the nature of passion...

Next thing she knew she was lying on the bed, her eyelids closed tight. She was listening to the rapid-fire beating of her heart. It seemed to be shaking her entire being. She lifted a hand to contain her wild heart, slowly opening her eyes.

Only to discover Clay was gone.

CHAPTER SEVEN

CLAY'S big 4WD hummed along the highway, its shadow racing after them. A heat haze rose off the never ending black ribbon of road, shimmering in the air in front of the bonnet. The Great Dividing Range that stretched five thousand kilometres from the tropical tip of Cape York in Far North Queensland to the magnificent stone ramparts of the Grampian Ranges in Victoria, loomed to their left, a formidable barrier between the lush eastern seaboard and the vast Outback. The dry, *dry*, land that had taken the lives of early explorers and many an adventurer without trace. Today the Range looked spectacular, Clay thought, its rugged slopes hyacinth-blue in the blazing heat. It was another brilliantly fine day and the huge Spinifex plains were beginning to reveal themselves in wild golds and greens with broad domed, stunted trees dotted here and there over the countryside.

They had long since left the beautiful Darling Downs region with its wonderfully fertile agricultural land, travelling through the fruit and wine zones, the golden Granite Belt and the cotton fields with their high yielding quality crop, out past the gas and oil regions into the real Outback and the sheep and cattle stations.

'Okay?' Clay asked, glancing down at the blond head stirring on his shoulder.

'Oh, I'm sorry!' Carrie straightened abruptly. 'I must have dozed off.'

'You did,' he smiled. 'That's okay. I liked it.'

'I didn't get much sleep last night,' she explained, putting a hand to the thick plait at her nape. That was an understatement. Apart from an initial hour or two she hadn't slept at all she was so overwrought.

'You're worrying about what's going to happen when you arrive home?'

Carrie nodded.

'The authoritarian father,' Clay sighed. 'I'll make sure I'm not like that. I hate to ask but doesn't your mother ever take your side?'

'Of course she does,' Carrie protested. 'She's a wonderful mother.'

'She makes up for your father's distant kind of parenting?'

'I've told you too much, Clay,' she said.

'You have to tell someone,' he said. 'Besides, I worked it out for myself.'

'Why did you go off and leave me?' she asked. 'Last night, why did you leave me?'

'Right now, Caroline, you're immensely vulnerable,' he said quietly. 'You have an ex-fiancé who betrayed you— He is *ex*, by the way?' He gave her a sidelong glance.

'I told him this morning,' she said. 'I know I said I wasn't going to until he was out of hospital, but I changed my mind after the events of last night. It was only the briefest visit to convince myself he was physically, at least, on the mend. And he is.'

'What did he say?'

'Nothing. He expected it. Why wouldn't he?' she said without bitterness.

'Just checking,' Clay replied. 'I know what a tender heart you have. I left you, Caroline, because I just can't bear to do anything to hurt you. By the same token it was the *hardest* thing I've ever done.'

'I was beginning to think I was frigid,' she said.

He laughed aloud. 'Well, you got *that* wrong. You're *perfect* to make love to.'

'Maybe I never knew what making love meant,' she said.

Just under an hour later they were driving over a grid beneath the huge sign supported by two massive posts that marked the entrance to the station. Victory Downs.

Carrie shifted uneasily in the passenger seat. She hated confrontations but she knew there was one coming up. As for Clay who drove so calmly and efficiently beside her, it was as he said—he was well able to take care of himself.

They swept along the wide driveway lined by magnificent she-oaks. Flocks of woolly white sheep were off in the distance. Kangaroos hopped leisurely towards the silver line of the creek. An eagle soared overhead. Station horses grazed in the home paddocks.

Home. But for how much longer? She didn't understand why her father was leaving the station to her cousin Alex and she never would. It almost seemed as if he were telling her to get married or get thrown out! Her father's delight in her engagement seemed to perfectly express his feelings.

After about a mile they came on the homestead.

The dominating double storeyed central section, the original house, was Georgian in style but single storey wings had been added on later. The whole effect was of order and serenity. The paint on the decorative shutters gleamed as it did on the white ornamental wrought iron. The homestead and the surrounding lawns and gardens, irrigated by bore water, were beautifully maintained—in sharp contrast to the tremendous neglect the once 'Princess of the Western Plains' Jimboorie House had suffered. Carrie loved her home, but in her eyes it lacked the sheer sweep and romance of Jimboorie.

'Here we go!' Clay said, laconically, bringing his 4WD to a halt in the shade of a spreading bauhinia.

Around the side of the east wing two splendid Scotch collies came flying, their long silky near orange coats streaming in the wind.

'Here, boys!' Carrie called, patting her knees.

Clay's handsome face lit up. 'What beautiful creatures!'

'Prince and Blaze,' Carrie told him proudly. 'You won't get better than them. They're working dogs. They'll be pleased to meet you.'

'I'll be pleased to meet them.'

Excitedly the dogs welcomed Carrie home, then turned to sniffing the newcomer who bent to scratch one then the other behind the ear. 'Shake hands.' Clay gave the order to the older dog, Prince.

'He mightn't do it. He doesn't know you—' Carrie broke off laughing, as Prince obediently presented Clay with a paw.

'Good boy!'

Carrie looked past Clay to see her mother coming down the verandah steps towards them. 'You're home, darling,' she called, her face wearing a welcoming smile. 'Good trip? Clay, how nice to see you again.' Smilingly Alicia put out her hand to this stunning young man who so recently had entered their lives like a comet.

'How are you, Mrs McNevin?' Clay responded, shaking hands and looking down into Alicia's beautiful face, that scarcely bore a trace of ageing. Caroline was destined to look like this in maturity, he thought. He had been introduced to the McNevins briefly after he had won the Cup. Alicia had been gracious to him then, but he hadn't expected the friendly greeting he was getting now.

'I'm well, thank you, Clay,' Alicia said. 'I'm sure you'd like to come in and have something to eat after that long trip.'

Carrie's eyes sought her mother's. 'Where's Dad?' she asked carefully.

Alicia was totally relaxed. 'He and Harry Tennant have flown off to Longreach for a meeting. Your father won't be back until tomorrow afternoon.' In other words, the all clear. 'Come into the house,' she invited. 'It's hot standing in the sun. So how did you find Scott?' she asked Carrie as they walked towards the homestead, the dogs trotting quietly by their side.

'It's all very upsetting, Mamma,' Carrie said. 'Didn't Thea Cunningham get in touch with you?'

Alicia smiled tersely. 'She certainly did. I'm not sure now if I didn't tell her off, poor woman. She idolises that boy. In a way she's ruined him. But enough of that. Come in and freshen up then we can sit and relax.'

Clay stayed on for an hour of conversation that skirted any difficult issues. Afterwards both women saw him off.

Alicia slipped an arm around her daughter's waist as they walked back to the house. 'Do you know, I can't remember when I met such a charming young man. And so well spoken. I like him very, *very* much.'

'You liked Scott, remember?' Carrie pointed out with a touch of irony.

Alicia's beautiful eyes clouded. 'I had no idea he was so full of deceit.'

'You haven't heard the half of it, Mamma,' Carrie said.

'Good God there's not more?' Alicia asked in dismay. 'Thea couldn't wait to recount your meeting outside the restaurant in Toowoomba. She said Clay threatened to knock Bradley down. I must confess that shocked me though sometimes I think Brad Harper needs flattening.'

'I didn't think Mrs Harper told lies,' Carrie said, angrily. 'It was Mr Harper who threw a punch at Clay. He blocked it and told Mr Harper not to try it again. That was it!'

'She seemed to think *you* were to blame. You'd let them all down.'

They had reached the verandah. Now both sank into planter's chairs. Carrie looked straight ahead. 'Natasha is carrying Scott's child,' she said baldly.

Alicia who had eased back into her chair sat bolt upright. 'What are you saying?' She stared at Carrie, a dazed look on her face.

'Natasha's pregnant. Believe it,' Carrie repeated harshly.

A bewildered look passed across Alicia's face. 'What sort of an abject low life is he?' she demanded to know.

Carrie sighed deeply. 'I daresay Natasha contrived it. Needless to say with his help. She's mad about him.'

'Dear God!' Alicia shook her head slowly from side to side. 'I take it his parents don't know?'

'I wouldn't like to be Scott when he tells them.' Carrie bit on her lip hard. 'Mr Harper would be a pretty violent sort of man once he gets going. He loves Scott, but he expects him to toe the line. Scott, by the way, told Natasha to have an abortion.'

'That was his solution, was it?' Alicia asked in utter disgust. 'Get rid of his own child? God, haven't *you* been lucky? And haven't your father and I been colossally stupid? You're well out of it.'

'You think I don't know that?' Carrie said. 'Dad thought Scott was perfect for me. He'll be shocked. Does he know Clay was with me in Toowoomba?'

'No, and we won't tell him,' Alicia said.

'Is that a good idea?'

'It's the best one I can think of at the moment.'

'I should probably tell the truth. Dad runs too much of my life.'

'He means well, Carrie,' her mother said. 'He'll be really upset about the whole sorry business. But it's Scott who's the villain here, not Clay. Your father has to get over his misconceptions.'

Carrie considered. 'He's too rigid in his ways. I don't think he's ever going to approve of Clay. He's set his mind against him.'

'Not so different to how he treated Clay's father,' Alicia said in a tight voice. 'But what the heck! You're a woman now. You can do as you please.'

'Maybe the day will come when *you* can, too, Mamma.' Carrie said meaningfully and closed her fingers around her mother's.

When Carrie returned to the homestead at noon for a bite of lunch—she had teamed up with the vet doing his morning rounds—her father had returned home. She could hear his voice upraised in anger as she mounted the front steps. Her father rarely raised his voice. It simply wasn't necessary. Arguments with his wife were exceedingly rare, but they were having one humdinger of an argument now.

Carrie hesitated, uncertain whether to go back outside or find her way up to her bedroom through a side door.

'How could he *do* this? How could he spoil everything,' Bruce McNevin was asking in a rage. 'Here you are able to wind any man—any man at all—around your little finger and Carrie can't hold onto her own fiancé. I thought she'd be married in December. I thought we'd have our lives to ourselves.'

'What a dreadful thing to say, Bruce,' Carrie heard her mother reply, her voice full of pain.

'All right I'm sorry. I've done my best, Alicia. God knows I've tried. But she's not *mine*. How can you expect me to love her? I've tried all these years to love her but I *can't*. She's not my blood. Why do you think I've left the station to young Alex. He at least, *is*.'

Carrie reached for something to hold on to.

Click, click, click! It all came together. *She's not mine!*

A trembling began right through her body. A profound sadness filled her eyes. Nonetheless, she didn't step backwards, but forwards. She was devastated, but to her wonderment, not demolished. *She's not mine!* Hadn't such a thing been implied by his behaviour all these years?

'Shut up and keep your voice down,' Alicia ordered in a voice akin to the sharp crack of a whip. 'Carrie will be home soon.'

'She's home *now.*' Carrie found herself in the kitchen, where her parents or her mother and the man she thought was her father faced each other across the table like combatants in a deadly battle. 'Would someone like to explain to me what I just overheard?'

Alicia's face went paper-white. 'Carrie, darling!' She rushed to her daughter who stood stricken but resolute in the open doorway.

Carrie held up her hand, warding her mother off. 'Who exactly am I, Mum? Is there anyone in this world who hasn't betrayed me? My father all these long years isn't my father at all. So *who* is? I'm not going anywhere until you tell me.' Her dark eyes bore into her mother's. 'That's if you *know*?'

Bruce McNevin stood watching Carrie with such an odd look on his face. 'Please don't speak to your mother like that,' he said. 'I'm sorry you had to hear that. I'm just so terribly upset.'

'*You're* upset?' Alicia rounded tempestuously on her husband, unleashing one of her stunning tennis backhands. 'You miserable bastard!' she cried. 'You miserable whining cur! You *swore* you'd never tell her.'

Bruce McNevin stood as stiff as a ramrod against the blow, the imprint of Alicia's hand clear on his cheek. 'I didn't tell her. She overheard. This was just supposed to be between you and me, Alicia.'

'God!' Alicia moaned. 'I don't want to live with you anymore, Bruce. You've killed whatever feeling I had for you. Carrie is my daughter. I love her best in the world. Far more than I could ever love you.'

'But you never loved me, did you?' Bruce McNevin's grey eyes glittered strangely. 'I've been the one who's done all the loving.'

Carrie intervened, saying what she had to say as if it were enormously important. 'You don't know the first thing about love. You don't even know about simple compassion. You're a cold man. You think only of yourself. God, it must have been so hard for you fathering a child that wasn't yours. Why didn't you tell Mum to have an abortion?'

A white line ringed Bruce McNevin's tight mouth. 'She *wouldn't* have it, that's why!'

Alicia shook her head, her eyes full of grief. 'Never, never!'

'So who's my father, Mum?' Carrie ignored the tears pouring down her mother's face. 'Or is it as I said. You don't know.'

'She's knows all right,' Bruce McNevin burst out furiously. 'But she couldn't marry him. He was married already. I was the poor fool who took her to the altar.'

'It was all you ever wanted.' Alicia rounded on her husband with utter contempt.

'I loved you then. I love you now,' Bruce McNevin's grey eyes turned imploring.

'Totally amazing!' Alicia gave a broken crow of laughter. 'You actually believe it. This marriage is *over,* Bruce. All these years I've lived with your emotional blackmail. Now it's out in the open.'

His answer was full of fear. 'You don't mean that. You'll never leave me, Alicia. It would be very wrong and dishonourable. I've been good to you, haven't I? I've tried my best with Carrie, but the way she looks at me! It's like she's always *known*.'

'I guess some part of me did,' Carrie said. 'Now I don't give a damn which one of you leaves. All I need to know is the name of my real father, then I'm out of here.'

'Where to? You have nowhere to go.' Alicia made another attempt to take her daughter in her arms, but Carrie would have none of it.

'Oh, yes, I have,' she said.

'I hope you're not talking about Cunningham?' Bruce McNevin's breath escaped in a long hiss.

'None of your bloody business,' Carrie said, enunciating very clearly. 'Who's my father, Mum. I *must* know.'

'You're crazy!' Bruce McNevin said.

'Shut up, Bruce!' Alicia looked positively dangerous. She turned her head towards her daughter. 'I can't tell you, Carrie. Maybe one day.'

'One day very soon.' Carrie was adamant. 'Understand? Now tell the truth if you can, Mamma. Did my *real* father know about me?'

Alicia's white face flushed deeply. 'I never told him.'

'He had a right to know.'

'Yes, he did,' Alicia admitted, revealing the depth of her old anguish.

'What would he have done, do you think?'

'He'd have bloody well wrecked his marriage,' Bruce McNevin suddenly shouted. 'A *good* marriage, mind you. Two small children. Two boys. I never had a son,' he cried, his voice full of bitterness.

'Nothing wrong with *me*, Bruce,' Alicia said. 'You never would see a doctor.' She turned her attention back to her daughter. 'I couldn't tell your real father I was pregnant, Carrie. I couldn't do it to him,' she confessed, brokenheartedly.

'No, but you could do it to *me*,' said Carrie. 'That makes you a ruthless person. I should hate you, Mamma. I'm not sure I don't right now. You were supposed to protect me. Not deliver the two of us up to this man.' Her gentle voice was harsh.

Alicia collapsed into a chair, crumpling up over the table. 'Please don't go, darling. Don't leave me,' she sobbed. 'We'll go together.'

Carrie shook her head. 'You have your husband. You've stuck it out with him all this time. I *am* going to find my father. With or without your help.'

'He'll never recognise you as his daughter,' Bruce McNevin told her, the expression on his face half scorn for Carrie, half misery for himself. 'Not even now when his wife is dead. Scandal can't touch a man like that.'

'Oh, yes, he will.' Alicia's tears abruptly turned off. 'I know that much about him.'

'Then perhaps when you're ready you'll give me his name,' Carrie said. 'I don't intend to embarrass him. I just want to see him with my own eyes.'

'You have seen him, you little fool!' Bruce McNevin had totally lost his habitual cool. One side of his face was paper-white, the other flushed with blood. 'All you have to do is watch television.'

'What's he talking about, Mum?' Carrie asked.

'Go ahead. Tell her,' Bruce McNevin dared his wife.

'Is he some television personality?' Carrie asked with something like amazement.

'No, no, nothing like that!' Alicia shook her head. 'He's an important man, Carrie.'

'Oh, listen to her! He's an *important* man. And I'm not?' Bruce McNevin glared at his wife.

'Oh, shut up, Bruce,' she said yet again. 'I wish to God you'd just been *kind*. I'll tell you when I'm ready, Carrie. Please don't ask me now.'

Carrie could see the trembling in her mother's hands. 'Okay,' she sighed, her heart torn. 'Now I hope you don't mind if I throw a few things in a bag. It won't take me long. I'll get the rest of my things picked up.'

'Carrie, no!' Alicia jumped up, her voice full of emotion. 'Please stay. We'll work something out.'

'Not anymore, Mum.'

'Let me handle this, Alicia,' Bruce McNevin said, striding after Carrie as though she were deliberately causing her mother unnecessary pain. 'Where are you going, Carrie? Answer me.'

'Sorry, Mr McNevin.' Carrie turned with great severity on the man she had called father. 'You've given your last performance. You've waited for this a long time. You wanted me out? Be thankful. I'm going!'

When she arrived at Jimboorie, a red sun was sinking towards the jewelled horizon. Carrie stepped out of her 4WD, which one of their employees had brought back from the town only that morning, looking up at the great house. There was the glow of lights inside. She had parked right at the base of the flight of stone stairs, now she leaned into the vehicle keeping her palm pressed flat on the horn.

I'm on the run, she thought. *I'm a fugitive. A profoundly wounded woman.*

At least Clay was at home. She felt in her jeans pocket for the folded note paper she intended to present to him. He would understand what it was. It was her response to the advertisement for a wife he'd never placed. Surely he'd told her she would fit the bill? She had nowhere else to go. And nowhere else she wanted to be.

Clay's tall rangy figure appeared on the verandah. 'Caroline, what's up?'

She gave him a pathetic little wave, feeling pushed to the limit, yet in the space of a nanosecond the vision of herself as a child waving to him while Clay, the handsome little boy, waved back flared like a bright light. For weeks and weeks she had searched the archives of her mind for that cherished memory. Now like some miracle it presented itself, bringing her a moment of happiness.

Clay lost no time covering the distance between them, moving through the portico and taking the steps in a single leap.

'I've just remembered waving to you when I was a little girl. Isn't that strange?'

'Strange and beautiful,' he said, staring down at her 'That meant a lot to me, Caroline.' He spoke quietly, gently, seeing her disturbed state. 'What's happened?'

She looked up at him a little dazedly. 'I've left home and I'm never going back.'

He absorbed that without comment. 'Come inside the house,' he said, tucking her to his side. 'You're trembling.'

A parched laugh escaped her lips. 'How come nothing shocks me to the core anymore?'

'You're *in* shock, that's why,' he pointed out, already feeling concern he could have been a cause of the family fallout.

From somewhere furniture had appeared in the drawing room; a huge brown leather chesterfield and two deep leather armchairs. A carved Chinese chest acting as a coffee table stood on a beautiful Persian rug all rich rubies and deep blues. She looked at the comfortable arrangement with a little frown on her face. 'Where did these things come from?'

'Out the back,' he said, offhandedly. 'There's more in store in Toowoomba. So are you going to tell me?' He led her to an armchair, waited until she was seated. 'What happened? Did you have an argument with your father?'

'What father?' she said.

Clay's face darkened. 'He surely couldn't have told you to go?'

Carrie shrugged. 'No, I did that all by myself.'

'Look, would you like coffee?' Clay suggested. 'I've got some good coffee beans. Won't take me a moment to grind them and put the percolator on.'

'I'll come with you,' she said, her movements almost trancelike.

Furniture had been moved into the enormous kitchen as well. It hadn't been there on her visit. He really was settling in. A long refectory table adorned the centre of the room with six carved wooden chairs, Scottish baronial, arranged around it, three to each side. The seats were upholstered in luxurious dark green leather. The huge matching carver stood at the head of the table. 'Expecting guests?' she asked, starting to drag out one chair. God, either it was *heavy* or she had lost her strength.

'*You're* here,' Clay pointed out, directing her to the carver instead, with its substantial armrests. A big man, it suited him fine. It nearly swallowed her up.

'This is a marvellous kitchen,' she said, looking around her. 'Or it could be. These chairs really belong in a dining room, you know.' She ran her hands along the oak armrests. 'Were they shipped out from England? They're antique. Early nineteenth century, I'd say.'

'Plenty more where they came from,' he said, busying himself setting out china mugs. 'While you were visiting Harper, I took a look at what was in storage. My favourite things were still there. Things I remember from when I was a child. There'll be more than enough to furnish the ground floor. I don't know about upstairs. Twelve bedrooms takes a bit of furnishing. At least I have a bed.'

'That's good,' she said wryly. 'Somewhere to rest a weary head. You might want to take a look at this.' She stretched her right leg so she could remove the folded notepaper from the pocket of her tight fitting jeans.

'What is it? Hang on a moment, I'll just grind these beans.'

Carrie covered her ears, counting to about twenty.

A few moments later, the percolator on the massive stove, Clay took the seat right of her. 'So what's this?' He unfolded the crumpled paper, looking at it with interest.

'It's not my best effort. I just had enough time to get down the facts,' she explained, very carefully, very precisely.

He turned his head to stare into her large, almond eyes. She was hurting badly but she wasn't going to say. 'Is this what I think it is?'

'Read on,' she invited, with an encouraging little movement of her hand.

He began again. 'This is truly *remarkable,* Caroline,' he said when he had finished. 'On the scale of one to ten, I'd give you an eleven. No, wait, a twelve!' He refolded the letter and thrust it into his breast pocket.

'Isn't it good,' she agreed. 'I mean it's so good you won't need to advertise for anyone else.'

'Well, that will certainly save a lot of time,' he said briskly. 'It's all happening around here. I have a firm lined up to fix the roof and a team of tradesmen to do the repairs. They'll be kept busy for months. There's an expert on the environment—a Professor Langley, my old professor—calling some time soon to advise about drought and flood management on the station. He's brilliant. He's bound to know someone to restore the garden.'

'Good heavens, you have been busy.' For a few moments he had completely taken her mind from her own problems. 'Where's all the money coming from?'

'*You,*' he said.

She caught the gentle mockery in his eyes. 'I don't come with a dowry, Clay,' she said sadly. 'I daresay I'll be cut out of my ex-father's will without delay. I do have a little nest egg from Nona. That's my grandmother, Alicia's mother. I wish Nona were here, but she went to live in Italy after my grandfather died. You're welcome to that.'

'Why how very sweet of you.' Clay lightly encircled her wrist. 'But such a sacrifice isn't necessary. That money is *yours.* Don't feel bad about not coming with a dowry. I told you Great-Uncle Angus was far from broke. In fact he'd have given Scrooge a run for his money.'

'So he left you the money as well.'

'I guess I was the only one he could think of.' Clay's comment was sardonic. 'One way or another we have enough.' He lifted her hand and kissed it.

'How upset that's going to make your relatives!' Carrie, numb for hours, awoke to sensation. 'They were hoping it was all going to fall down around your ears.'

'Instead of which I get to marry the princess and share the pot of gold,' he said, gazing deeply into her eyes. 'Now tell me what's causing all this suffering? Take your time.'

'Mum had an affair before she was married.' She spoke in a voice utterly devoid of emotion.

Clay's strong hand closed over her trembling fingers. What was coming next just had to be momentous.

'The man I *thought* was my father all these years isn't my father at all.' Carrie gave him a heartbreaking smile. 'Can you beat that?'

'How could they do that to you?' Clay felt the blood drain from his own face.

Carrie shrugged. 'Apparently he was married with two kids, but he wasn't worried about committing adultery. Neither was Mum. He must have been Someone even then. Mum decided she couldn't break up his marriage. She married Bruce McNevin instead.'

'So that explains it,' Clay said, steel in his voice.

'At least Mum didn't consider a termination.'

'Thank God for that!' he breathed, unable to contemplate a world without Caroline. 'So how did this all come out? I mean what provoked it after all these years?'

She pulled a sad little clown's face. 'You know the old saying. Eavesdroppers never hear well of themselves? I could hear them arguing when I arrived back at the house for lunch. They *never* argue. I heard my *father* say, "She's not mine! How can you expect me to love her? She's not my blood!"'

Muscles flexed hard along Clay's jawline. 'Go on. You have to get this off your chest.' He stood up to pour the perked coffee, setting a mug down before her then moving the sugar bowl close to her hand. 'Do you want milk or cream?'

'Black's fine.' She spooned a teaspoon of sugar into the mug and absently began to stir.

'Have another teaspoon of sugar,' he urged. 'You're awfully pale. Wasn't your mother worried about your driving?'

Carrie nodded. 'She begged me not to go but I couldn't stay in *his* house another moment. He's only tolerated me because of Mum. He's still madly in love with her. So what the hell's wrong with *me?* Am I so unlovable?'

Clay felt a rush of anger on her behalf. 'That's the last thing you have to worry about,' he said so emphatically she felt immensely relieved.

'You *really* want to marry me now? I could turn into a pure liability. Well?' she pressed, directly holding his eyes. 'Answer me, Clay.'

'You aren't going to *order* me to marry you, are you?' he asked gently.

'Not unless you want an illegitimate bride. Mum wouldn't even tell me who my real father is. *He* knows.'

'Who, McNevin?'

'Yes. Don't worry, I'll find out.'

'Then what will you do?' he asked very seriously.

'I don't mean to embarrass my real father, Clay,' she explained carefully. 'I just want to lay eyes on him. Can you understand that?'

'Caroline, God!' He was debating whether to pick her up and carry her upstairs. If ever a girl needed loving it was this beautiful traumatised young creature. 'Of course I understand. It's hard to feel *whole* when you only know the identity of one parent.'

'My entire childhood and adolescence lacked *wholeness*,' she said, painfully aware that was so. 'I think I'll be content once I know who my real father is. I can watch him without his being aware of it.'

'What if you're not? What if you're impelled to go up to him and tell him he's your father? He'd have to remember your mother so he'd have to know who *you* are. You resemble her greatly.'

'Clearly I resemble her physically, but not in other ways,' Carrie said, carefully. 'I can't believe she's lied to me all these years. Couldn't she have concocted another story? Couldn't she have married someone else but Bruce McNevin? He's a *mean* man at heart. How could anyone disavow a baby, a little girl, a dutiful daughter?'

'It's no excuse, but I suppose he felt tremendously insecure about your mother,' Clay suggested. 'She's obviously never loved him.'

'Then why didn't she divorce him?' Carrie shot back.

'I can't find an acceptable answer, Caroline.' He stared at her, his eyes full of compassion. 'Who knows what goes on inside a marriage anyway? He must have been doing something right.'

'Not by *me*! But he thought he was the perfect husband. I've even heard him say so.' Carrie picked up her coffee mug again. 'This is good.'

'When did you last eat?' he asked, his eyes moving over her inch by inch.

'Breakfast.' She shrugged. 'I was coming in for lunch when my whole life was shattered. Soon as I heard their voices I knew something awful was going to happen. I think he's actually relieved it's all out in the open. He no longer has to pretend.'

'Should I ring your mother and tell her you're with me?'

'No, Clay, *no*!' She laid a restraining hand on his tanned arm.

'Whatever she's done or *had* to do she loves you, Caroline. She'll be frantic.'

'Don't worry, she won't kill herself,' Carrie said, her voice as dry as ash. 'She knows where I am anyway. I mightn't have told her, but she'll guess. Even my dear old ex-father, guessed I was heading here. That's three ex's in my life. Ex-mother, ex-father, ex-fiancé.'

'Your mother's always your mother, Caroline,' he said. 'Nothing's going to change that.'

Carrie released the gold clasp at her nape so her hair fell heavily around her face. 'Do you realise if all this miserable business with Scott hadn't happened I probably would never have found out?'

'It has occurred to me,' Clay said, thinking however desperate she felt she looked absolutely beautiful. The purity and symmetry of her small features transcended mere prettiness.

'We've all been living a lie,' she said in a melancholy voice. 'I could have married Scott in a few weeks' time.'

'I imagine Natasha would have had something to say about that,' he said dryly.

'Lord, you'd think the accident and all the stress would have triggered a miscarriage.'

'You didn't want that to happen?'

'Oh, my God, no. Dear God, no,' Carrie said. 'Natasha's tough and her baby's tough. They'll have to be. Do you mind my burdening you with all this?'

'Mind, how? Haven't you applied for the position of my wife? I have your application—which I will frame—in my pocket.' There was tenderness on his face and a shadow of physical yearning kept under tight control.

'Well, I don't much care for anyone else,' she said. 'So what's the answer? Or do you want to hear from more women?' She didn't realise it but she sounded incredibly anxious.

'Yours was the winning application,' he said.

'The *only* application.'

'I won't hold it against you. Now as soon as we settle you in I'll have to think about feeding you. By a stroke of good fortune I stocked up the last time I was in town.'

She shook her head. 'I'm not hungry, thank you all the same, Clay.'

'Well *I* am.' He stood up. 'I won't feel happy eating alone. And now I think of it, you didn't mention in your application if you could cook?'

'And you didn't ask.' She smiled weakly. 'I can cook. My mother taught me. I'll never be as good as her. You know *he* didn't want a housekeeper. We have Mrs. Finlay from town come in once a week to do the cleaning. He didn't want *anyone* but Mum I can see that now. And Mum acted as though she *owed* him. What for? For his marrying her when she was pregnant? Is that what Natasha will have to settle for?'

'Don't upset yourself,' Clay said. 'Harper and Natasha will have to solve their own problems.'

Carrie's heart stuttered.

She sat straight up in bed, saying shakily, 'Who's there?'

She looked about her in a dazed panic. Where *was* she?

She waited for full consciousness to kick in. Thank God! She was at Jimboorie with Clay. He had given up his bed for her, a brand-new king-sized ensemble, electing to spend the night in the massive four poster—too big to ever be shifted—in the bedroom just across the hall. They had shared a bottle of red wine over a dinner of tender beef fillet, tiny new potatoes and aspara-gus—all cooked to perfection by him—and the alcohol had soothed her sending her off to sleep.

The effects had evaporated. She didn't know what time it was but something had awoken her. She willed her memory back to an image.

A slow opening door? A shape of a woman? She was sure it was a woman. Jimboorie House was haunted. Clay's mother had seemed to think so.

Calm down, fool that you are.

Hold down panic. Control the mind. It was only a dream.

She lifted a glass of water from the bedside table; sipped at it, panning her eyes around the huge room, listening intently for the slightest sound. Outside in the night, a full moon was riding high in the indigo sky, its rays washing the room with a silvery light.

But it was impossibly dark in the far corners. A strangeness seemed to be in her and at that moment a supreme wakefulness. She didn't quite know how to handle it. Or herself. One thing she did know with absolute certainty was, she couldn't lie in the semidarkness anymore. She couldn't bear to be alone, either. She wanted love. Plenty of it.

She rose from the bed in that unquiet night, catching the scent of gardenia that wafted from her nightgown She always used gardenia sachets amid her under garments and nightgowns. Her Thai silk robe bought in Bangkok was at the end of the bed, the white background scattered with bright red poppies, the edges bound with ebony. She slipped it on, tying the sash loosely. Her heart was aching afresh as the events of the day flooded back to her mind.

At long last she knew what her inner being had always suspected—the man whose name she bore wasn't her father. All he was, was her mother's husband. Twenty-three years of lying. Could she ever forgive her mother for that? Slowly she made her way across the room, heart fluttering, keeping to the band of moonlight.

What was her excuse for going to him? What would she say when he woke to find her standing beside his bed, staring down at him?

Love me, Clay. I desperately need to be loved.

Need had overtaken her entirely. She felt no embarrassment. just the driving need for comfort that only he seemed able to give.

His door was open. Carrie could hear his gentle, even breathing. She glided as silently as a shadow across the floor towards that massive bed. His naked back was turned to her, one shoulder raised high. She loved the shape of him, the shape of his broad shoulders, the way his strong arms could enfold her. She loved everything about him. And she wanted to learn more. Fate had carried her here to this moment, to this beautiful man. Her life had slipped out of focus. He had the power to put it back in place.

She held her flowing hair back with her hand. 'Clay!'

She thought he might take moments to stir but he was instantly alert.

'God, Caroline!' Fast breathing now. He sat up, thrusting a hand through his hair. 'I was dreaming about you.'

'Isn't it better I'm here?' She let her voice fall to a whisper.

'Did something frighten you?' he asked, with concern. 'I could have sworn you'd sleep through the night.'

'Isabelle's ghost,' she said and even laughed. 'She must walk around the house at full moon. May I get into bed with you?'

'Caroline.' Instantly he was aroused, every nerve throbbing. He dared not think what would happen if she did. 'You know what that means?' he managed to say. 'I couldn't possibly resist you. I just *couldn't*. I'm not strong enough.'

'But I don't want you to resist me,' she said. 'I want you to touch me. I want to touch you.' She reached out and moved her fingers, gently, slowly, over his broad chest letting them tangle in the fine mat of hair.

Clay felt his blood come to a rolling boil. 'Caroline!' he said, taking hold of her wrists. 'What are you trying to do to me?'

'You want me, don't you?'

I want you to be mine forever! 'It's for your protection,' he said, valiantly holding her off, at the same time desperately trying to exert the full force of his will. 'I would let you stay with me. I want nothing more in the world than have you stay with me, but I'm worried. I'm worried about *you*. What might happen.'

'Stop worrying,' she said, pulling away from him gently, to slide off her robe. Then she clambered onto the high bed. 'Can't you understand, Clay. I *need* loving.'

Why tell him *that* when he was wild for her! The very enormity of having her there in the bed beside him, inhaling her fragrance, all but robbed him of his precious self-control.

'So you're going to allow me to take your virginity?' He was already utterly aroused and unable to do a damn thing about it.

'Isn't that your wish?'

'I want you to give it to me. I don't want to *steal* it from you. I care about you too much.'

'Well, I can't wait,' she said. 'I *thought* I wanted to wait. I could have waited easily with Scott. But not with you. It's not all about sex, Clay,' she said reaching out to stroke his face. 'I want *you*. I need you. It's as simple as that.'

'And it has to be this very night, my little runaway Caroline?' he asked with immense tenderness, staring down at her.

'Only you can save me from the pain.'

The blood rushed to his head. She thought herself safe with him. She *was*. But he had to be so gentle when the adrenaline was roaring through his body. He tried to slow himself down by kissing first the side of her neck, then the exquisite little hollow in her throat, moving back to her eyes, her cheeks, her nose, then her lovely mouth. He kissed her again and again, until they were both light-headed, his hands moving irresistibly to her breasts, creamy like roses, their pink tips flaring at his touch. While she moaned softly he let his hand slide down over the smooth tautness of her stomach, downward yet to her secret sex.

Her mouth formed words. She exhaled them.

'My true love,' she said.

It was an utterance that reached right through to Clay's soul.

And he was gentle with her, his fingers feathering over her, his mouth following...

'Do you like that?' He wasn't going to do a thing that didn't give her pleasure.

'Perfect!' she moaned, her back arching off the bed.

'You are *so* beautiful!' He turned her over, making long strokes over her satiny back, cupping her buttocks so smooth and round, pressing his lips to them...

She was yearning for him to move into her, her body was demanding release, but he continued to work his magic on her, inch by inch.

She kept her eyes closed tight.

When he gently worked her clitoris, she made a wild strange sound, like a bird keening. The sensuality was profound. Wonderful and unbearable at the same time. She was panting and gasping with excitement, reaching for him frantically, guiding him to the entrance of her sex.

'Yes!' she cried, overcome by the extraordinary piercing sensations that were running riot in her body. She couldn't control them. They were controlling her.

Clay drew back, laying his palms flat on the bed to either side of her. 'I'll be as gentle as I can,' he vowed.

'You're a *magician*,' she whispered back.

'Am I?'

'*Yes!*' She was desperate for him to push into her. To *fill* her.

There was a twinge of pain. No more. Then a spreading rapture like life giving rain spreading over the flood plains.

'You're okay?' he whispered urgently against her cheek, striving to keep his own driving needs reined in.

'I *adore* you!' she cried.

Was there ever an answer that could please a man more? He threw his head back with sheer joy and she arched up to kiss his throat. 'Adore you. Adore you. Adore you!'

He couldn't hold back a moment longer. Not after that. Their bodies radiated heat and an incredible *energy*. The whole room was filled with it. It crackled like live wires.

He plunged into her in an ecstasy of passion and she met that plunge, spreading her silken thighs for him. It thrilled him to the core. She was spreading herself wide-open to him, her soul as naked as her beautiful body. His heart swelled with pride, exultation, and an enormous gratitude. He felt *free*. Unburdened of the griefs that had long plagued him.

Neither of them held back. They gave of each other unstintingly. At long last they had discovered something they had never known before.

Pure Desire. Pure Love.

CHAPTER EIGHT

CLAY and Carrie were coming back from a long ramble down to the creek, when they saw Alicia's Land Rover make a sweep around the circular driveway and park, bonnet in, to the shade of the trees. There had been a fantastic, wonderfully welcome downpour of rain around dawn, which had awakened them to more glorious love-making, and now the whole world was washed clean.

'It's Mamma,' Carrie said, unnecessarily, holding Clay's hand tight.

'I'm sure she's only come to see if you're all right,' Clay said, calming her. 'Take it easy, Caroline. Your mother must be under a lot of stress.'

Alicia was waiting quietly on the terrace.

'Why have you come, Mamma?' Carrie started in at once, though her heart smote her at the unhappiness in Alicia's face.

'I *had* to come,' Alicia said.

'Please sit down, Mrs McNevin.' Clay held a chair for her. 'How are things at home?'

'Not good, Clay,' Alicia said, releasing a long sigh. 'And please call me Alicia.'

'I'd be happy to,' Clay said quietly. 'Let's all take a seat.' He put his hand gently on Carrie's shoulder, exerting the slightest pressure. 'Would you two like to talk while I make coffee?'

'I'd be grateful for that, Clay,' Alicia said.

'No problem.' He strode away into the house.

'What a very considerate young man!' Alicia said, sighing as though she'd never had the good fortune to meet one in her life. 'I'm leaving Bruce,' she told Carrie.

'Isn't it about time?' Carrie asked. 'You don't love him, Mum. You've never loved him, have you?'

'Look,' said Alicia, 'give him some credit. When I knew I was pregnant with you I was absolutely desperate—'

'You couldn't tell Nona?' Carrie broke in, not understanding *her* nona was another person to her mother.

'I didn't think I could,' Alicia confessed. 'Your grandmother had—still has—very definite ideas about how a well-bred young lady should conduct herself. She would have been shocked and bitterly disappointed in me. The scandal would have been enormous. It wouldn't have been so bad if I'd been able to marry the father of my child, but I couldn't.'

'Then why have an affair with him?' Carrie asked, sounding stern about it.

'You're in love with Clay, aren't you?' Alicia made a plea for understanding. 'You're in love at last?'

Colour flooded Carrie's cheeks. 'Oh please…Clay's not married.'

'I was mad about him,' Alicia said. 'I truly believe he loved me. Neither of us planned it. It wasn't supposed to happen, yet all it took was a smile. We met at a fund-raiser. I knew who he was, of course—'

'Which is a damn sight more than I do,' Carrie interrupted.

'He noticed me from across the room.' All these years later Alicia's beautiful eyes went dreamy.

'He would. Any man would,' Carrie said, still in that critical voice.

'I'd noticed him back. That's how it started.'

'Easy as that, eh?' Carrie's voice was unwillingly sympathetic. 'When did you start sleeping together?'

'When did you start sleeping with Clay?' Alicia retorted.

'Last night,' Carrie admitted freely. 'And at dawn this morning. It was *wonderful*! Clay has restored my faith in humanity.'

'I hope you used protection?' Alicia went from penitent to concerned mother.

'I'm not going into details,' Carrie said. '*Why* have you come, Mamma? Your husband hasn't threatened you in any way?' The very thought frightened her.

'He's beside himself,' Alicia said.

'I'm quite sure he's blaming me for all this?' Carrie said.

Alicia passed on the answer. 'I want you to come with me to Melbourne, darling,' she said as though it were something both of them simply had to do.

'Melbourne? What for?' Carrie started to picture where her mother would go. To friends? To a hotel?

'For one thing you can't stay here with Clay,' Alicia pointed out quietly.

'Why not?' Carrie turned squarely on her mother. 'I'm going to marry him.'

'And he'll be a wonderful husband, I know.' Alicia took the news very calmly. 'But you want to do it right.'

'Unlike *you*!' Carrie was near tears. But her mother did have a point—Clay was now the owner of Jimboorie Station. He intended to work it. He intended to restore the homestead. He *was* a Cunningham. If nothing else she had to uphold *his* reputation. 'What's in Melbourne?' she asked finally.

Alicia looked sightlessly across the grounds. 'Your *father*,' she said.

'You're back!' Bruce McNevin greeted his wife the moment she walked into the homestead. 'I knew you'd come back. You've got nowhere else to go.'

'I'm only here to do a little packing, Bruce,' Alicia said. 'I'm taking Carrie with me to Melbourne.'

He blocked her way as she walked to the stairs. 'Just how long do you think you can stay with friends?'

'I've almost lost touch with them, haven't I, through you? Let me past, Bruce.'

'Not until we have this out. I'm extremely unhappy with your behaviour, Alicia. You *owe* me. As for Carrie, she's just going from bad to worse. I suppose she was with Cunningham?'

'Why don't you ask them?' Alicia said. 'They're waiting for me in the driveway.'

'They're what?' Bruce McNevin hurried to the front door, looking out. 'How dare they!'

'They don't trust *you* to behave yourself, Bruce.'

'Have I ever laid a finger on you?' He strode back to her looking outraged.

'If you had, I'd have found the guts to move on.'

Bruce McNevin shook his head, something like grief in his eyes. 'I *knew* Leyland's child would split us one day. You surely can't be going to him? You have no place in his life.'

'I know that, Bruce,' Alicia said simply, 'but Carrie does. There have been a lot of changes in society since I was a girl. People are more *accepting*. Carrie wants to meet her father. I'm going to arrange it. Neither of us intend to embarrass him though I know he'll be deeply disturbed.'

'And what about his sons? What are they going to think?'

Alicia spread her hands in an inherited gesture. 'There are secret places in everyone's life. Besides, they're married men now. Or one is.'

'Been checking up on them, have you?' McNevin sneered.

'They're a prominent family, Bruce. The media like to report on prominent families.'

'They'll relish *this* scandal then, won't they? The return of the prodigal ex-lover along with their lovechild. And what about your oh so proper mother? What the hell is she going to think?'

'She's a long way from here, Bruce. I can't worry about her anymore. Or about you. I'm not the panic-stricken girl I once was.'

'My God!' McNevin breathed. 'I love you, Alicia. Doesn't that mean anything to you anymore?'

She met his eyes directly. 'It would have meant a lot had you loved my daughter, too!' Alicia went around him and mounted the stairs.

Clay and Carrie sat waiting for Alicia to reappear. 'I think I should go in,' Clay said. It was he who had insisted on accompanying them back to the homestead, concerned Bruce McNevin might react badly when faced with losing the woman he loved.

'It's all right, Mum's coming out onto the verandah.' Carrie breathed a great sigh of relief. 'She's ready for you to collect the luggage.' They watched Alicia give them a signal then walk back into the house.

Clay restarted the engine. 'I'll drive up to the steps. He might come out, Carrie. Be prepared.' For *anything,* Clay thought, glad he was with them. Even the mildest man could turn dangerous given enough provocation.

Clay was out of the Land Rover when Bruce McNevin strode out onto the front verandah, his manner highly confrontational. 'Ah, it's *you,* just as I thought. I want you off my land, Cunningham,' he ordered.

Clay reacted calmly to the blustering authority. 'I certainly don't want to be here, sir. But Mrs McNevin needs a helping hand.'

'Not from the likes of you,' Bruce McNevin said, suddenly producing a whip.

'I wouldn't think of using that,' Clay warned. 'You'll definitely come off second best. I understand you're upset, Mr

McNevin, but don't push it. I'll just collect what luggage Mrs McNevin needs then we'll be on our way.'

'*Where,* may I ask?' Bruce McNevin said in his most pretentious voice.

'There's plenty of room at Jimboorie.'

'That crumbling heap!' McNevin scoffed.

'You won't know it in six months' time,' Clay assured him. 'Jimboorie House will in time be restored to its former glory. Take it from me.'

'You!' McNevin asked with great sarcasm. 'What, that wicked old bastard leave you a few bob, did he?'

'Actually he did,' Clay confirmed casually. 'He was far from broke as you seem to think. What he was, was a *miser.* Heard of them?'

Bruce McNevin's face was a study. 'You're not *serious*?'

Clay nodded. 'Yes, I am. Excuse me, sir. I'll just collect those bags.'

Clay entered the house without incident. Bruce McNevin waited a moment then stalked down the steps and over to the Land Rover.

Seeing him coming Carrie opened the passenger door and stepped out onto the gravel to confront him.

McNevin's face was dark with anger. 'I'll never forgive you, Carrie, for what you've done.'

'I haven't done anything,' she said. 'It's more what was *done* to me. I have to live with the fact my own mother lied to me all these years. I suppose she *had* to, to stay under your roof. Your precious reputation is very important to you, isn't it? But she had to pay dearly. I was to be passed off as your child, but right from the beginning you never treated me as family, much less an adopted daughter. You mightn't be able to see my scars. They're not visible to the naked eye, but they're there. Things might have been very different had you been a man of heart.'

Bruce McNevin flushed violently. 'I know I fed you, clothed you, housed you, educated you. Don't let's forget all that, my girl. You never wanted for anything.'

'Maybe so and for that I thank you, but I went wanting for a bit of affection,' Carrie said quietly. 'I know you couldn't make it to love. You couldn't love another man's child.'

'How many men do you think could?' he asked with the greatest impatience. 'All those cuckolded men, when they find out through DNA the child they've long parented isn't theirs at all, doesn't the love switch off? You bet it does. That bastard, that father of yours, raped your mother.'

For the first time in her life, Carrie literally saw red. Clouds of it swirled in front of her eyes, almost obscuring her vision. Even now he couldn't leave well enough alone. He was impelled to cause more damage. Blindly she moved a step closer to the man who had treated her all her life with such contained severity and cried out. 'That is absolutely unforgivable. And a blatant *lie*. Your miserable mean way of getting even? I demand an apology.'

'Why, you arrogant little girl!' Bruce McNevin exclaimed, quite shocked by her anger. 'To think you can *demand* anything of me.'

Carrie's heart was thudding violently in her chest. 'It's normal enough in parent-child interactions but then I'm *not* your child, am I? My poor mother is *still* in love with that man even today. There was no rape as well you know. No need when they were madly in love with each other.'

'What a mess! What a bloody mess!' Bruce McNevin groaned, burying his face in his hands.

'A mess that has to be straightened out.' Carrie swept her thick plait back over her shoulder. 'I doubt if I'll be seeing you again, Mr McNevin. So I'll say my goodbyes. I feel sorry for you in a way. But I shouldn't. I can only remember my life as your daughter as being *loveless*.'

Her mother and Clay were already out of the house and coming towards them. Now they joined her, Alicia standing close beside her daughter.

'If you must do this, do it, Alicia,' Bruce McNevin addressed his wife, ignoring Carrie and Clay. 'No good will come of it, I warn you.'

'Well it wouldn't be *you* if you wished us luck,' Alicia said in an ironic voice.

'I don't want you upset and embarrassed, Alicia,' he said. 'I repeat. I love you. I've stood by you no matter what. I'm not perfect. I didn't have it in me to take to another man's child. I'm not proud of it but it's understandable. The thing is I've always stood by you. Take all the time you want, but come back to me. *Please!* We have a good marriage.'

'And you think we'll have a better one without Carrie?' Alicia asked.

'I'm *sure* of it,' he responded.

'Please, Mamma, let it be,' Carrie intervened, glad of Clay's rock-solid support at her back.

'I suppose you think this puts you in the picture, Cunningham?' Bruce McNevin exploded, as he could see his whole life changing. 'Scott's out of the way, so you move in?'

'I don't see that that's any of your business, Mr McNevin.' Clay's tone was perfectly even. It was evident he had no intention of being goaded. 'I'll say good day to you.'

'And good riddance!' Bruce McNevin shouted as Clay moved off. 'Make sure you never come on to my land again.'

'You should take it easy for a while, sir,' Clay advised, half turning and looking over his shoulder. 'You could have a stroke, heart attack, anything.'

'Mind what he's saying, Bruce,' Alicia warned her husband. 'The blood has mounted into your face.'

'So why should I care?' he cried in a distraught voice. 'You're leaving me, aren't you?'

Alicia's beautiful face looked incredibly sad. 'There's nothing left for us, Bruce. I should have done this a long time ago but I didn't have the courage to start again. Our marriage never had a firm foundation. I take a lot of the blame. I'll see a solicitor in Melbourne.'

'To start divorce proceedings?' He closed his eyes then looked up to heaven.

'Of course.'

His expression entirely changed. 'Then don't think for one moment you'll get your hooks into *my* money. *You're* the guilty party. I'll make sure everyone knows that. Mark my words, Alicia, you start this and I'll fight you every inch of the way.'

'Bruce. Goodbye,' Alicia said.

Senator Leyland Richards was having a busy morning. He had flown in from Canberra, the seat of Federal Government, to Melbourne, his home town, the previous evening and he hadn't had a moment to himself since.

Ah, well, this was the life he had wanted, wasn't it?

Fame and fortune.

He sighed deeply, putting off a phone call he knew wouldn't wait. Though his plans, as yet, weren't in the public domain, it was his intention to quit politics after giving twenty-five years of his life to it. He had discussed the matter privately with the Prime Minister; they had agreed on the best time for the announcement and he had received a strong message he was a definite contender for the top diplomatic posting to Washington.

'You're just the man for the job, Leyland!' The P.M. had assured him.

The thing was, though it was far from apparent to his family, his friends, his parliamentary colleagues *and* the P.M. he had lost the driving ambition that had set him on the high road to success. Son of a wealthy legal family—he had himself worked for a few years as a barrister in the prestigious law firm established by his grandfather—his entry into politics was put on the fast track when he married Annette Darlington, the only daughter of Sir Cecil Darlington, a senator at that time. It was in the way he had handled a tricky matter for the Senator that had really brought him to Darlington's attention. From then on it had been plain sailing. He was given to understand Sir Cecil was very impressed with him and his style. Meetings were arranged to interest him in running for a blue ribbon seat he eventually won. Annette, so very sweet and earnest, fell in love with him. And that was that! It was a union of *old money*. A union of Establishment families. The beginning of a good marriage and highly successful career in politics.

It had been two years now since he had lost Annette to breast cancer, a great blow. Annette had made him a wonderful wife and had been a loving mother to their two sons. She had wanted nothing more than to serve him and the boys. Most men would have found that an enormous bonus but he had secretly wanted *more* from her. More of *herself*. He had always been regarded as the perfect husband and son-in-law. God knows he had always tried to be. Less than a year after the untimely death of Annette, the retired Sir Cecil who had adored his only daughter, had suffered a massive heart attack while they were out on his yacht, *Lady Annette II*. Leyland had had an ambulance waiting as they docked, but his father-in-law had died before they reached hospital. Two great blows in as many years.

He'd done his duty by everyone. Doing one's duty was extremely important. Now he felt, despite the honours that apparently were yet in store for him, he desperately needed time to himself. Time to breathe. To sit in the sun. Take the boat out. He was fifty-three now. Surely it was time for a sea change? As it was he was at everyone's beck and call. Only an hour ago his press secretary had popped her head around the door to remind him of a press interview she had lined up for the following morning.

He made the phone call to the Shadow Minister in the Opposition who he definitely didn't admire, but as a natural diplomat he was able to get his message across to the extent a date was made for a round of golf at the weekend. At least the man was a fine golfer.

He was working diligently at some papers when his secretary buzzed him.

'I know you didn't want to be disturbed, Senator,' she said in a low, confidential tone, 'but there's a lady here—she has no appointment—who thinks you might see her.'

A lady? *What* lady? There were no ladies in his life since he'd lost Annette, but plenty who'd like to replace her. 'What's her name, Susan?' he asked. 'What does she want?' Dammit, he didn't really have the time.

'A Mrs. Alicia McNevin, Senator,' Susan said in hushed tones. 'She claims to be an old friend. She's very beautiful.'

Leyland felt something like an electric shock go through him. *Alicia! My God! Would the memory of her ever fade?*

'Send her in, Susan,' he said.

Carrie was so nervous she was almost ill. And she missed Clay terribly. He had become her rock and her refuge.

'Are you *sure* he wants to see me?' she begged her mother.

'He sent the limousine for us, didn't he?' Alicia gently smiled and took hold of her daughter's trembling hand. 'We're having dinner with him at his home, which he intends to hand over to his elder son and young family. Lee has bought a penthouse apartment with fantastic views of the city, Port Philip Bay and the Dandenongs. I understand it's undergone a brilliant renovation. We'll get to see it.'

'You call him Lee?'

'I always called him Lee,' Alicia said.

'And what am I going to call him?' Carrie swallowed hard.

'Just relax, darling,' Alicia advised. 'It will come. Lee is a most charming man. He will put you at ease.'

'Will he now?' Carrie said. 'That remains to be seen. And he wasn't angry you never told him about me?' Her voice was quite shaky, but she so desperately needed reassurance.

Alicia glanced through the window of the moving Bentley, the uniformed chauffeur separated from them by a glass panel, which went up and down at the touch of a button on the console in front of them. 'Well, you know, darling it's as I told you. He was extremely shocked and very upset. But he rallied.'

'It's a wonder he didn't throw you out,' Carrie murmured, imagining the scene.

'That wouldn't have been at all like him.' Alicia shook her golden head.

Tonight she looked even more beautiful than usual in a sophisticated champagne coloured silk and lace blouse over a tight black skirt, her still small waist cinched with a wide black belt. She'd had her hair done and she radiated a womanly allure on a level her daughter had never seen before.

'I'm sorry he lost his wife.' Carrie's mind was inevitably drawn to the *wife*. She wondered whether Annette Richards had known about her mother. She hoped not.

'He loved her,' Alicia said simply, though her heart twisted.

'Does he know about *you*?' Carrie asked. 'Does he know you're going to divorce Bruce?'

'He knows *everything*!' Alicia said.

Carrie's mouth was so dry she didn't know if she was going be able to speak. This was her *father* she was about to meet. Her *real* father, her own flesh and blood. Her mother, on the other hand, looked remarkably relaxed. Alicia was obviously looking

forward to the evening. She had gone to some lengths to look marvellous. Carrie had never laid eyes on her outfit. What had gone
on at that meeting? Carrie wondered for the umpteenth time.

Impressive wrought-iron gates led to the Richards mansion,
a Tuscan style residence that had known functions and parties
galore. The house was designed over four levels, drawing
Carrie's eye upwards. Impressive as it was, it lacked the sheer
breadth, the size, the glamour of Jimboorie House, falling down
or not. Garden beds lay to either side, clipped in the classical
style. The gates were open in welcome and the chauffeur guided
the Bentley into the huge garage to the right.

'We're here, darling,' Alicia said, touching a hand to her hair.
'You okay?' She was clearly anxious. Carrie looked lovely but
austere, like a little saint facing martyrdom.

'I'm fine.' Carrie tilted her chin, wishing Clay were there so
she could hold his hand. 'Lead on.'

They stood outside a magnificent front entrance door for barely
a moment. It swung open revealing a stunning reception area
with tall marble columns and a double staircase with beautiful
black and gold balustrading leading to the mezzanine level. It
usually stopped most people in their tracks but Carrie saw none
of it. Her eyes were rivetted on the tall charismatic man who
stood staring down at her, so deeply, so gravely. She had seen
him many times on television and in the newspapers never
dreaming there could be any possible connection, now she saw
him in the flesh before her.

My father! My God!

The realisation didn't come easily. He looked what he was: a
powerful, brilliant person, but how would he react to her? Would
he entertain her briefly then send her on her way? He had the sons
he wanted. The life he wanted, albeit as a widower. Perhaps not
for long. Would he swear her to secrecy? A man in his position

would surely be desperate to avoid a scandal? Would this meeting even have been possible had his wife still been alive?

She saw him reach out to take her mother's hand. She saw her mother reach up to kiss his cheek, a *special* kiss. 'Lee, this is your daughter,' Alicia said, tears falling gently from her eyes.

Leyland Richards looked down at that lovely, strained young face with its beautiful, haunted doe eyes. despairing that they could never find their lost time. But there was the future! He lifted his arms wide, not making the slightest attempt to hide the raw emotion in his eyes. Indeed his handsome face was suddenly ravaged by a mixture of joy and anguish. This was his daughter. He knew instantly and without doubt.

'Caroline!' he cried. 'Oh, God!' The very breath seemed to catch in his throat.

An enormous lightness seized her. Nothing could hold her back now. This was really her father. She had waited twenty-four years for this. Carrie went into those outstretched arms, feeling them close strongly around her. 'That's my beautiful girl!' her father said.

CHAPTER NINE

I COULD lose her!

Two weeks went by before Clay started tormenting himself with that frightening prospect. Each day she sounded more and more as though a wonderful new world had been opened up for her. Which of course it had. Her father had done what *he* couldn't. This was what he feared. She was happy living a life apart from him. And it could go on. Perhaps forever! Her biological father hadn't had a moment's hesitation in acknowledging her, she'd told him with enormous gladness in her voice. Clay loved her, so he was able to share in her happiness. But, Lord, he needed her as much as her father. *More.*

Miracles do happen, Clay!

He'd thought one had happened to him. But she was only going to keep him posted. She had been through bad experiences what with Harper, then Natasha and finally the man she had all her life called Father. He'd caught her at a vulnerable moment in time when she was emotionally fragile. That's why she had come to him— actually putting it down on paper—that she would marry him. Maybe now she thought of her promise as just plain *craziness.*

It occurred to Clay in acknowledging her, her father stood to lose much of his unsullied reputation. He would have to know that. His was a household name. Caroline's father was Senator

Leyland Richards, leader of the Upper House. Clay, though not overly struck on politicians of any persuasion, had always admired the man. He was a handsome, distinguished, highly intelligent, highly articulate with a magnetic charm that drew people to him. Senator Richards had long had the reputation for being a man the people could trust. He was also a natural diplomat with an engaging wit that worked well for him in his televised interviews. Women loved him. He got their vote. In short he was just the sort of man Caroline should have had as a father right from the beginning.

Caroline had told him in confidence that Senator Richards intended to retire from politics at the end of the year when he would make his announcement. Who was I going to tell anyway? Clay thought. Bruce McNevin, who must be cursing the day he ever opened his mouth? Clay went over their conversations a hundred times in his head. All too often the line was bad. A lot of work was being done around Jimboorie so he could only take calls at night. Caroline had been gone such a short time, yet she had already met her half brother, Adrian and his wife and young family. The younger brother, Todd, who had won a Rhodes Scholarship to Oxford, was overseas. They were well on the way to becoming one happy family.

Alicia, too, had been welcomed with open arms. Of course Alicia was a stunning woman. Clay was human enough to wonder if Caroline and her mother would have been received so magnanimously had both of them been ordinary people and plain to boot.

By the end of the third week Clay found himself going about his business grim-faced. He missed her unbearably. She may have found her *real* father, but she was in *his* blood, too. He prayed she'd remember that. Absence either made the heart grow fonder or the fond memories faded. Not that she didn't always tell him how much she missed him when she called. But when was she coming home? And where *was* home? He was so lonely without her. He had never known such loneliness. He told himself repeatedly he could scarcely begrudge her this precious time with her father. He was just so worried she might want to stay close to him. Hell, was that so unusual?

Clay worked so hard in an effort to take his mind off his anxieties, he fell into bed each night exhausted to the bone.

By the end of the month he decided to take action. He didn't have to watch every dollar anymore. He would take a trip to Melbourne. He would buy a decent suit and go calling, courting, whatever. Caroline and her mother had moved out of their hotel into the Richards's residence. He had the telephone number and the address. He was hurting so badly he just *had* to see her. If she wanted to remain in Melbourne with her new family he had to face the appalling fact there was *nothing* he could do about it. The very thought made him flinch. Without Caroline, all his plans for the future would be smashed.

They were all over him in the department store where he went to buy some smart city clothes. There was no question it would be extremely easy for a bush bachelor to find plenty of female company in the city but getting a one of them to leave the city for the lonely isolated Outback was another story.

In the end he bought much more than he needed, but the staff seemed hell-bent on outfitting him in a way they considered appropriate. He might have been a sporting icon—they made such a fuss.

You have the most wonderful physique, Mr. Cunningham. Those shoulders!

Thank you, ma'am.

A male staff member, scarcely less flattering, gave him the name of a top hairdresser and how to find the salon. Okay, his hair *was* too long and too thick!

He didn't know himself. He stared in the full-length hotel mirror wondering if he hadn't gone too far. What a change an Italian suit made. Was it really worth an arm and a leg? Where would he ever wear it again? But never mind. He had to look right for Caroline. They hadn't cut all that much off his hair. Just trimmed it and somehow shaped it so it followed the line of his skull. All those people trying to take care of him! He was glad he'd been able to frame his sincere thank yous.

In the hotel foyer he had to be aware he was turning women's heads. He could have laughed aloud. He was no sex symbol. He doubted if they would have looked at him in his usual gear of bush shirt, jeans and high boots. He didn't get the truth of it. He was a stunning-looking man, but he never saw himself that way.

His longing for Caroline was like a hand stretched out to guide him. He had decided on surprising her, not sure she would be at home, but willing to take the chance. She'd told him the Senator was always extremely busy sorting out his affairs but he always managed to make it home for dinner. Why not, with two beautiful women waiting for him! Maybe the Senator and Alicia would revive their doomed romance. They must have loved one another at one time though it would have been a sad thing to break up a marriage, especially when small children were involved.

He took a taxi to the Richards's residence, pausing a moment on the street to look up at the Italianate mansion, four storeys high. The lot would have fitted neatly inside Jimboorie House, he thought, with a surge of pride for the old historic homestead. The workmen he had hired had been going at the renovations hell for leather. It was astonishing what they had already achieved though there was a great deal still to be done. It would all take time and money. With Caroline by his side he had looked on it as a glorious challenge.

A sweet faced maid called Loretta answered the door, telling him Miss Carrie was relaxing by the swimming pool at the rear of the house. She stepped back smilingly to allow him to enter the house. He returned the smile, telling her he didn't wish to be announced. It was a surprise visit. He would walk around the side of the house to the pool, coming on Caroline that way. Loretta grinned at him like a coconspirator.

Following her directions he took the paved path on the western side of the house. A lot of the plants growing to either side were unknown to him. The character of the front and side gardens seemed very classical to his eyes. It was all very beautiful, very orderly, but the only splash of colour was white. Even the flowering agapanthus were white. Clay rounded the end of the rear terrace looking towards a spectacular turquoise swimming pool. The smooth surface was flashing a million sequinned lights. The pool was edged by towering royal palm trees and plushly upholstered chaise longues. A short distance back was a large open living area shaded by a terra-cotta roof with a deep overhang supported by substantial columns. The space was luxuriously furnished with circular tables, rattan armchairs and long rattan divans, again upholstered in an expensive looking fabric.

Sitting on one of the divans, their heads close together, were Caroline and a good-looking young guy, dark haired, bronze tan, wearing blue swim shorts. Clay took a deep calming breath. Then another. Caroline was wearing a brief swimsuit as well with a little bit of nothing over it. Her beautiful hair tumbled down her back. Her skin glowed honey-gold. Her lovely limbs looked wonderfully sleek.

His heart began thudding like Lightning Boy's hooves. He stood perfectly still, watching. Why wouldn't she attract eligible young men? God, hadn't he been struck by her allure, quite apart from her beauty, right off. Why wouldn't this guy who was staring into her face with what seemed to Clay tremendous intensity want her? They were, in fact, closely regarding each other.

Clay's stomach tightened into a tight knot. He braced himself as the guy placed a hand on her shoulder. He'd fallen in love with her. Of course he had. And Caroline was mightily interested in him. He felt lacerated by that.

I'll be damned if I'm going to let him take her away from me!

They were so close to each other. *Too* close. The guy said something that made Caroline laugh; a silvery, carefree peal of laughter.

Clay's built up feelings of anticipation evaporated like creek water in a drought. He was tempted to confront them, find out who this guy was, but he had the dismal idea he might finish up throwing the poor man in the pool. He'd rather die than act the jealous fool.

Clay turned on his heel and walked away. There was no longer any excitement. No longer the sheer magic of seeing her.

Barely ten minutes later Carrie, having had enough sun, was making her way back into the house when she met Loretta coming out onto the terrace.

'Enjoy your swim?' Loretta asked with a coy smile.

'It was lovely!' Carrie said, shaking back her hair

Loretta's gaze went past her to the pool. 'The gentleman didn't stay long,' she said in a disappointed voice. 'I was just coming down to see if you'd like refreshments.'

'Gentleman? What gentleman?' Carrie frowned.

'Why the young man who came to see you,' Loretta said, eyes wide. 'He was gorgeous!' she added.

'Did he give a name?' There was puzzlement on Carrie's face.

'Sure!' Loretta nodded. 'Couldn't forget it. A nice name. Suited him. Clay Cunningham. Didn't want me to announce him. Said it was a surprise. I directed him—'

Carrie's voice overlapped the maid's. 'What time was this, Loretta?' she asked, urgency in her manner.

Loretta considered, head to the side. 'Not more than ten minutes ago. He was walking around the side of the house to the pool.'

'Well, he never arrived.' He saw *us,* Carrie thought.

She waited not a moment longer. 'Loretta, tell my mother

when she comes home I've gone into town,' she called over her shoulder. 'Tell her I'll try to make it back for dinner.'

It took Carrie under twenty minutes to track down the hotel where Clay was staying, shower, dress and call a cab to take her into the city. Lee had made a car available to her but she didn't want to waste precious time trying to find a parking spot. When she arrived at the hotel she was told by reception Mr. Cunningham wasn't in his room. He had been seen going out perhaps an hour or so before. He hadn't returned.

Carrie retreated to a lounge setting in the spacious foyer ordering a cold drink. Where had he gone? What time was he coming back? Whatever time it was, she was prepared to wait. She was so consumed by her thoughts she almost missed Clay's arrival maybe a half hour later. What alerted her was the ribald comment of one of two young women sitting across from her, sipping highly coloured and decorated cocktails.

'Strewth, would you look at the guy who just walked in?' the one in the sequinned top gasped, putting down her glass and sitting bolt upright. 'Wouldn't I love to wrap my legs around him!'

'We have a Ten!' the other squealed, holding up all her digits.

Carrie's heart catapulted into her throat. She followed the focus of their gaze although it would have been difficult indeed to miss him. It was Clay. He looked absolutely stunning in his city clothes, his marvellous hair barbered to perfection. He had meant to surprise her. Instead, apparently, she had shocked him into leaving.

When the girls saw her staring so avidly, the one with the sequinned top called to her. 'Bet your life someone has already high-jacked him. Wanna come over and join us?'

Carrie stood up quickly, grabbing her handbag. 'Love to, but I can't, sorry. I have to catch up to my fiancé.'

'You mean that drop-dead dreamy hunk of a guy is your man?' the one with the scarlet hair asked.

'Sure is,' Carrie confirmed proudly.

'You're one lucky lady,' Scarlet Hair told her with a wicked grin.

Though she pursued him as fast as her high heels would allow, Carrie saw him disappear into a waiting elevator. She took the next available, glad she knew which floor and which room he was in. Even then he beat her inside his door

He came at the third knock.

'I missed you at the house,' Carrie said brightly, devouring him with her eyes.

He didn't respond, but stood looking down at her.

'Aren't you going to ask me in?' She had to duck under his arm to get into the room. 'What happened? Why did you leave?' She turned to face him.

He shut the door, leaned against it. 'One's the right answer and the other one isn't,' he said crisply.

'Fire away,' she invited, throwing her handbag down onto the bed.

'Right. One, I was running late for an appointment. Two, I thought I'd give that guy you were being so sweet to some swimming lessons.'

'You were *jealous!*' Carrie gave a little crow of disbelief.

He came away from the door abruptly, all six foot three of him, emanating radiant energy. 'What the *hell* did you expect me to be?' Despite himself Clay suddenly exploded. 'But, hey, I probably had no right. I mean it's not as though we're an old married couple or anything.'

'No,' she agreed, though her heart was fluttering. 'Why don't you try kissing me?' She threw it down like a challenge, moving right up to him and staring into his tense face.

'Why don't I?' He hauled her to him with one arm. 'I'm not enough for you, am I, Caroline?' His blue eyes were so full of emotion they *blazed.*

'I can't tell until you kiss me again,' she said.

He stared at her with those burning eyes, a frown between his brows. 'Do I look like a guy you can manipulate?'

'Manipulate?' She pretended to try the word out on her tongue. 'I don't know what that means!' She knew she was deliberately provoking him but excitement was running at the rate of knots. She was just so *thrilled* to see him and he didn't even know it.

'Of course you know what it means,' he countered harshly. 'Every beautiful woman knows *that*. I didn't aim for your love right off, Caroline. I hoped love would come. But I thought I had your promise. That little letter you wrote me. It said you wanted to be my wife.'

'Well, you didn't take it seriously, did you?' she flashed back. 'You haven't seen me for a month yet you can't even get around to kissing me.'

She actually sounded *aggrieved*.

Clay's strong arms trembled. He'd had enough of her mockery, sarcasm, whatever it was. This wasn't *his* Caroline— what had happened to her?—but he still wanted this Caroline. Madly. Badly. He couldn't look at her without wanting her. He couldn't inhale her fragrance. Clay gathered her up, unprotesting, and carried her back to the deep armchair where he settled her in his lap.

'Go on, kiss me,' she urged, her beautiful dark eyes staring into his, her long blond hair spilling over his arm.

His face tightened into a bronze mask. He wanted to pay her back. Yes, he *did*. But he could never hurt her. Instead he let his mouth move over hers, not punishingly, but letting it convey his deep need of her. His hands moulded her to him. He couldn't make sense of anything. He didn't try. It was the same old magic all over again. Magic that had the power to drain him of his bitter disappointment and anger.

When he finally lifted his head, he saw *radiance* on her face, though her eyes remained shut. 'Caroline?' Surely she couldn't kiss him like that and not love him?

'All right, you've kissed me,' she whispered, opening her dark eyes. 'Now tell me you love me.'

He was moved to reveal his heart. 'I love you,' he said, his voice a deep well of emotion. 'I want you to have my children. I'll love you until the day I die.'

Carrie was trying her hardest not to cry. She sat up a little, holding his face between her hands. 'So why didn't you trust me?' she reproached him.

He shook his head with regret. 'I will from now on, I swear! But God, Caroline, it was understandable, don't you think? I came on the woman I love staring into another man's eyes like he had the answer to all life's problems. A young good-looking guy who had his hand on your shoulder. We'll forget the fact both of you weren't wearing a lot of clothes.'

'Since when do you wear a lot of clothes when you go swimming, my darling?' Carrie asked. 'Haven't I rung you every night? Haven't I told you how much I missed you?'

'Not *enough* apparently,' he said, allowing a deep sigh to escape him. 'I took off before I embarrassed myself. And worse, *you.*'

'Let's face it, Clay,' she said gently, 'you made a mistake. Had you waited I could have introduced you to my half brother, Todd. When he heard about me, he decided on the spot he had to come home to meet me. He's only just arrived. I would have told you tonight.'

Clay threw back his head, stunned. 'Your half brother?' If only he'd phoned ahead he would have been told and saved himself a lot of heartache.

Carrie pressed her lips to his throat. 'My half brother,' she confirmed. 'I can't marry him but I can marry you.'

Clay stared at her until his raging emotions cut back to a simmer. 'I apologise,' he said finally. 'A man in love isn't entirely *sane.*'

'And I accept your apology,' she said, feeling giddy with sheer delight. 'I can't believe you're here with me.' To prove it she hugged him. 'About time, too.'

'And your new family?' Clay questioned, wanting to get things absolutely right. 'You're sure you don't want to stay close to them? We go back to Jimboorie, they'll be a long way away,' he reminded her.

'They're not going out of my life, Clay,' Carrie said. 'That's not going to happen.'

'Of course not,' he agreed, actually looking forward to meeting them. 'But you won't be able to see them on a daily basis or anything like that. There'll just be *me.*'

She took his hand in hers. 'I'm happy with that.' She smiled into his eyes. 'Hey, this reunion has been *perfect,* but my father and my half brothers have their own busy lives. Incidentally they all understand I love *you.* I've told them all about you. You have to meet them.'

'What right *now*?' Clay's voice was a low purr in his throat.

'No, not now.' She pulled down his head and kissed him lingeringly on the mouth. 'But tonight for dinner. I can't wait to show you off. Besides, I haven't quite forgiven you yet. You still have some work to do.'

'Okay,' he said in a smouldering voice, only too willing to prove his love.

'By the way.' Carrie deferred his ardent kisses for only a few seconds. 'We'd better get busy on our wedding plans.'

Clay laughed. 'I say we drink to that!'

'There's a bit more. If we don't, Mamma and Leyland are going to beat us to it, would you believe? Alicia is *still* Alicia, if you know what I mean.'

Clay smiled back at her. 'And Caroline is still Caroline,' he murmured, starting to seriously make love to her.

This was a wonderful outcome to all his hopes and dreams. One lonely bush bachelor had found himself the perfect wife.

EPILOGUE

Jimboorie House
18 Months Later...

THE army of tradesmen—roofers, carpenters, plumbers, plasterers, polishers, painters and wallpaperers, electricians—had all packed up and gone home. At some stage they would return—there was still plenty of work to be done on the many bedrooms of the upper level—but for now restoration work on the mansion had progressed so wonderfully well that Clay and Carrie had thrown it open to the people of the town and the outlying stations. Jimboorie House, once the hub of social life for the vast central plains of Queensland was set to take its place again as the reigning 'Princess' of the vast district's historic homesteads.

This particular gala day, a Saturday, had been set aside as a house warming for the very popular young couple whose splendid home it was and a fun day for all who had been invited. There was scarcely a soul—maybe one or two who had the sense to keep their resentments to themselves—who wasn't thrilled and proud to see 'the old girl' Jimboorie House rise like a phoenix from the ashes. This was *their* heritage after all. Guests were milling around the house now marvelling at what had been done. So absolutely *right*—Carrie and her mother, Alicia, had received hundreds of compliments and congratulations. They had worked closely with the decorators over the long months, demonstrating their own considerable artistic flair and innate good taste.

To Carrie, who couldn't quite believe in her own level of pure bliss, everything was a miracle. Finding Clay, her wonderful husband and her soul mate, was a miracle. Finding her real father another. The fact her and Clay's wishes for a baby had been granted was yet another glorious miracle. She had recently had her pregnancy confirmed. She and Clay were over the moon. So were Alicia and Leyland who had married quietly only a few months before. The fact Senator Leyland Richards had a beautiful daughter from an old twenty-year-plus liaison—the revelation had received wide media coverage—in the end proved no impediment to his diplomatic posting to Washington. Alicia and Leyland had, in fact, delayed their departure to attend the restoration party, making it clear they would visit at every available opportunity. Try to keep them away! Prospective grandparents, they were overjoyed by Carrie's news; Alicia promised she would return home for the birth.

Another stroke of good luck was that Bruce McNevin had very quickly consoled himself by taking a new wife, a rich socialite widow, still young enough to have a child. They were in fact on their honeymoon in Europe. Given their shared history and the fact they would be living in the same district, Clay and Carrie had decided, as they lived in an adult world, some kind of peace had to be made or at the very least an outward show of civility. Carrie hadn't the slightest doubt Bruce still loved her mother, but destiny had planned for Alicia and Leyland to be reunited at long last.

Carrie stood at the French doors looking out over the beautifully restored garden and the magnificent central fountain now playing, smiling quietly to herself.

'Now what's that little smile about?' Clay came up behind her wrapping his arms around her. Carrie was his *life*. Together they had made *new* life. He lowered his locked hands a fraction to press them lovingly against her tummy. 'Love you,' he murmured, the flame of desire never far from his blue eyes.

'Love you,' she whispered back, then gave a little ripple of laughter. 'See out there? I was hoping and praying Natasha and Scott would make a go of it.'

Clay looked out at the young couple who were the focus of her attention. Blond and raven heads together, they were pushing what had to be the Rolls-Royce of prams.

'Well it didn't happen overnight,' Clay remarked quietly, 'but it *is* happening, thank God. Natasha is certainly a different woman.' Natasha in fact had become a routine visitor to Jimboorie saying she was *family* all along.

'Motherhood suits her,' Carrie who was looking breathtakingly beautiful in her trouble-free early pregnancy observed. 'I was wrong all along about Scott. He wasn't going to turn his back on his child.'

'I don't believe his parents were going to let him.' Clay's retort was dry. 'But he seems determined to be a father. So good for him!'

'Well he has an excellent reason to get his life together,' Carrie said. 'Sean is a beautiful little boy.'

'And he'll have another cousin before long,' Clay said, bending his head to kiss his wife's satin cheek. 'God, how happy you've made me, Carrie!' he breathed. 'Supremely happy! You've even with your compassion turned Natasha into a friend. Not content with that, you've caused the Cunninghams to beg forgiveness for past wrongs.'

'It was *you* who did the forgiving,' she reminded him, enormously proud of her husband.

'How could I lock the old bitterness into my heart when I had such love in my own life?' he said simply.

Carrie's soft sigh was eloquent of her happiness. A special radiance emanated from her, visible for all to see. She pressed back against her husband's lean strong body, her head on his chest. 'And the greatest joy is yet to come,' she promised, placing her hands over his on her very gently rounded tummy.

'I didn't think it was possible for you to be more beautiful,' Clay whispered, 'but you *are!'*

And his voice was hushed with awe.

It wasn't until the gala day was drawing to an end that Clay was approached by a young man, around his own age, who thrust out his hand.

'It *is* Clay, isn't it?' The man smiled. 'Clay Dyson? Used to be overseer on Havilah a couple of years back?'

Clay's face broke into a warm answering smile as he recognised Rory Compton, scion of one of the wealthiest cattle families in the Channel Country deep into the southwest. 'Cunningham now, Rory,' Clay said as they shook hands. 'Cunningham is my real name, by the way. How are you and what are you doing so far from home? Not that it isn't great to see you.'

'Great to see you!' Rory responded with sincerity. He hadn't known Clay Dyson all that well, but what he had seen and heard he had liked. 'So what's the story, Clay? And this homestead!' He gazed towards it. 'It's magnificent!'

'It is,' Clay agreed proudly. 'There is a story, of course. A long one. I'll tell you sometime, but to cut it short it all came about through a bitter family feud. You know about them?'

'I do,' Rory answered with a faint grimace.

'Mercifully the feud has been put to bed,' Clay said with satisfaction. 'My great-uncle Angus left me all this.' He threw out his arm with a flourish. 'Caroline, that's my wife and I, have only recently called a halt to the renovations. They were mighty extensive and mighty expensive. What I inherited was a far cry from what you see now.'

'So I believe.' Rory nodded. 'I'm staying at the Jimboorie

pub. The publican told me about the open day out here. I'm glad I came.'

'So am I.' Clay's attractive smile lit up his features. 'Have you met Caroline yet?'

'The very beautiful blonde with the big brown eyes?' Rory gave the other man a sideways grin.

'That's Caroline.' Clay couldn't keep the proud smile off his face.

'I haven't had the pleasure as yet,' Rory said. 'I only arrived about thirty minutes ago, but I'm looking forward to it. You're one lucky guy, Cunningham!'

'*You* should talk!' Clay scoffed, totally unaware of Rory's current situation. 'How's Jay and your dad?' he said pleasantly.

'Jay's fine,' Rory said. 'He's the heir. My dad and I had one helluva bust-up.'

Clay could see the pain behind the level tone. 'That's rough! I'm sorry to hear it.'

'It was a long time coming,' Rory said quietly. 'The upshot being I didn't have much choice but to hit the road. I have some money set aside from my granddad. I guess he thought I might need it sometime. What I'm looking for now is a spread of my own. Nothing like Jimboorie of course. I'm nowhere in your league, but a nice little run I can bring up to scratch and sell off as I move up the chain.'

Clay looked into the middle distance, a thoughtful frown between his brows. 'You know I might be able to help you there,' he said slowly, already turning ideas over in his head. He knew of Rory Compton's reputation as a highly skilled cattleman with more vision than his dad and his elder brother put together. 'Why don't you come back inside. Meet Caroline. Stay to dinner. You're not desperate to get back to town are you?'

'Heck, no!' Rory felt a whole lot better in two minutes flat. 'I'd love to stay if it's okay with your beautiful wife?'

'It'll be fine,' Clay assured him. 'Caroline will be pleased to meet you. And we'll both have time to catch up.'

'Great!'

Destiny has an amazing way of throwing people together.

* * * * *

Look for Rory Compton's story coming soon.

Louise Valentine is still smarting from the humiliation of being fired from Bella Lucia by her workaholic cousin Max, and the discovery that she was adopted as a child. Then, Max turns up on the doorstep of her successful PR and Marketing company, insisting that she do some promotions work for the family's restaurant chain. At first Louise coldly rebuffs him—but then she finds that years of secret longing for Max cannot be forgotten so easily...

Here's an exclusive extract...

"So why are you so anxious to have me come and work for you?"

Because he was crazy, he thought.

Who did he think he was kidding? Working with Louise was going to try his self-control to its limits.

He took a slow breath.

"I want you to work *with* me, Lou, not *for* me. I respect your skill, your judgment, but we both know that I could buy that out in the marketplace. What makes you special, unique, is that you've spent a lifetime breathing in the very essence of Bella Lucia. You're a Valentine to your fingertips, Louise. The fact that you're adopted doesn't alter any of that."

"It alters how I feel."

"I understand that and, for what it's worth, I think Ivy and John were wrong not to tell you the truth, but it doesn't change who or what you are. Jack wants you on board, Louise, and he's right."

"He's been chasing you? Wants to know why you haven't signed me up yet? Well, that would explain your sudden enthusiasm."

"He wanted to know the situation before he took off last week."

"Took off? Where's he gone?"

"He was planning to meet up with Maddie in Florence at the weekend. To propose to her."

"You're kidding!" And when he shook his head, "Oh, but that's so romantic!" Then, apparently recalling the way he'd flirted with Maddie at the Christmas party, she said, "Are you okay with that?"

He found her concern unexpectedly touching. "More than okay," he assured her. "I was only winding Jack up at Christmas. It's what brothers do."

"You must have really put the wind up him if he was driven to marriage," she said.

"Bearing in mind our father's poor example, I think you can be sure that he wouldn't have married her unless he loved her, Lou."

Or was he speaking for himself?

"No. Of course not. I'm sorry."

Sorry? Louise apologizing to him? That had to be a first. Things were looking up.

She laughed.

"What?"

She shook her head. "Weddings to the left of us, weddings to the right of us and not one of them held at a family restaurant." She tutted. "You know what you need, Max? Some heavyweight marketing muscle."

"I'm only interested in the best, Louise, so why don't we stop pussyfooting around, wasting time when we could be planning for the future?" The thought of an entire evening with her teasing him, drawing out concessions one by one, exacting repayment for every time he'd let her down, every humiliation, was enough to bring him out in a cold sweat. "Why don't you tell me what it's going to cost me? Your bottom line."

"You don't want to haggle?"

Definitely teasing.

"You want to see me suffer, is that it? If I call it total surrender, will that satisfy your injured pride?"

Her smile was as enigmatic as anything the Mona Lisa could offer. "Total surrender might be acceptable," she told him.

"You've got it. So, what's your price?"

"Nothing."

He stared at her, shocked out of teasing. That was it? A cold refusal?

"Nothing?" Then, when she didn't deny it, "You mean that this has all been some kind of elaborate wind-up? That you're not even going to consider my proposal?"

"As a proposal it lacked certain elements."

"Money? You know what you're worth, Louise. We're not going to quibble over a consultancy fee."

She shook her head. "No fee."

Outside the taxi the world moved on, busy, noisy. Commuters crossing en masse at the lights, the heavy diesel engine of a bus in the next lane, a distant siren. Inside it was still, silent, as if the world were holding its breath.

"No fee?" he repeated.

"I'll do what you want, Max. I'll give you—give the family—my time. It won't cost you a penny."

He didn't fall for it. Nothing came without some cost.

"You can't work without being paid, Louise."

"It's not going to be forever. I'll give you my time until…until the fourteenth. Valentine's Day. The diamond anniversary of the founding of Bella Lucia."

"Three weeks. Is that all?"

"It's all I can spare. My reward is my freedom, Max. I owe the family and I'll do this for them. Then the slate will be wiped clean."

"No…"

He didn't like the sound of that. He didn't want her for just a few weeks. Didn't want to be treated like a client, even if he was getting her time for nothing. Having fought the idea for so long, he discovered that he wanted more, a lot more from her than that.

"You're wrong. You can't just walk away, replace one family with another. You can't wipe away a lifetime of memories, of care—"

"It's the best deal you're ever likely to get," she said, cutting him short before he could add "of love…"

"Even so. I can't accept it."

"You don't have a choice," she said. "You asked for my bottom line; that's it."

"There's always a choice," he said, determined that she shouldn't back him into a corner, use Bella Lucia as a salve to her conscience, so that she could walk away without a backward glance. Something that he knew she'd come to regret.

Forget Bella Lucia.

This was more important and, if he did nothing else, he had to stop her from throwing away something so precious.

"That's my offer, Max. Take it or leave it."

"There must be something that you want, that I can offer you," he said, assailed by a gut-deep certainty that he must get her to accept something from them—from him. Make it more than a one way transaction. For her sake as much as his. "Not money," he said, quickly, "if that's the way you want it, but a token."

"A token? Anything?"

Her eyes were leaden in the subdued light of the cab, making it impossible to read what she was thinking. That had changed. There had been a time when every thought had been written across her face, as easy to read as a book.

He was going into this blind.

"Anything," he said.

"You insist?"

He nodded once.

"Then my fee for working with you on the expansion of the Bella Lucia restaurant group, Max, is…a kiss."

* * * * *

Don't miss this sizzling finale to
The Brides of Bella Lucia
Liz Fielding's
THE VALENTINE BRIDE (#3934)
out in February 2007

Find out whether Max and Louise can put their turbulent past behind them and find a future together.

In February, expect *MORE*
from

HARLEQUIN

Romance

as it increases to six titles per month.

What's to come...

Rancher and Protector

Part of the

Western Weddings

miniseries

BY JUDY CHRISTENBERRY

The Boss's
Pregnancy Proposal

BY RAYE MORGAN

Don't miss February's
incredible line up of authors!

nocturne™

**WAS HE HER SAVIOR
OR HER NIGHTMARE?**

HAUNTED
LISA CHILDS

Years ago, Ariel and her sisters were separated for
their own protection. Now the man who vowed
revenge on her family has resumed the hunt, and
Ariel must warn her sisters before it's too late.
The closer she comes to finding them, the more
secretive her fiancé becomes. Can she trust the man
she plans to spend eternity with? Or has he been
waiting for the perfect moment to destroy her?

On sale December 2006.

HARLEQUIN® *Romance*®

What a month!

In February watch for

Rancher and Protector
Part of the Western Weddings miniseries
BY JUDY CHRISTENBERRY

The Boss's Pregnancy Proposal
BY RAYE MORGAN

Also in February, expect
MORE of what you love
as the Harlequin Romance line
increases to six titles per month.

REQUEST YOUR FREE BOOKS!
2 FREE NOVELS PLUS 2
FREE GIFTS!

HARLEQUIN ROMANCE

From the Heart, For the Heart

YES! Please send me 2 FREE Harlequin Romance® novels and my 2 FREE gifts. After receiving them, if I don't wish to receive any more books, I can return the shipping statement marked "cancel." If I don't cancel, I will receive 4 brand-new novels every month and be billed just $3.57 per book in the U.S., or $4.05 per book in Canada, plus 25¢ shipping and handling per book and applicable taxes, if any*. That's a savings of over 15% off the cover price! I understand that accepting the 2 free books and gifts places me under no obligation to buy anything. I can always return a shipment and cancel at any time. Even if I never buy another book from Harlequin, the two free books and gifts are mine to keep forever.

114 HDN EEV7 314 HDN EEWK

Name	(PLEASE PRINT)	
Address		Apt.
City	State/Prov.	Zip/Postal Code

Signature (if under 18, a parent or guardian must sign)

Mail to the **Harlequin Reader Service®**:
IN U.S.A.: P.O. Box 1867, Buffalo, NY 14240-1867
IN CANADA: P.O. Box 609, Fort Erie, Ontario L2A 5X3

Not valid to current Harlequin Romance subscribers.

Want to try two free books from another line?
Call 1-800-873-8635 or visit www.morefreebooks.com.

* Terms and prices subject to change without notice. NY residents add applicable sales tax. Canadian residents will be charged applicable provincial taxes and GST. This offer is limited to one order per household. All orders subject to approval. Credit or debit balances in a customer's account(s) may be offset by any other outstanding balance owed by or to the customer. Please allow 4 to 6 weeks for delivery.

Your Privacy: Harlequin is committed to protecting your privacy. Our Privacy Policy is available online at www.eHarlequin.com or upon request from the Reader Service. From time to time we make our lists of customers available to reputable firms who may have a product or service of interest to you. If you would prefer we not share your name and address, please check here. ☐

HR07

HARLEQUIN *Presents*

Welcome back to the exotic land of Zuran, a beautiful
romantic place where anything is possible.

**Experience a night of passion
under a desert moon in**

Arabian Nights

Spent at the sheikh's pleasure…

Drax, Sheikh of Dhurahn, must find a bride for his brother—
and who better than virginal Englishwoman Sadie Murray?
But while she's in his power, he'll test her wife-worthiness
at every opportunity….

TAKEN BY
THE SHEIKH
by Penny Jordan

Available this February.
Don't miss out on your chance to own it today!

www.eHarlequin.com

HPAN0207

REQUEST YOUR FREE BOOKS!
2 FREE NOVELS PLUS 2
FREE GIFTS!

H A R L E Q U I N   R O M A N C E®

From the Heart, For the Heart

YES! Please send me 2 FREE Harlequin Romance® novels and my 2 FREE gifts. After receiving them, if I don't wish to receive any more books, I can return the shipping statement marked "cancel." If I don't cancel I will receive 4 brand-new novels every month and be billed just $3.57 per book in the U.S., or $4.05 per book in Canada, plus 25¢ shipping and handling per book and applicable taxes, if any*. That's a savings of over 15% off the cover price! I understand that accepting the 2 free books and gifts places me under no obligation to buy anything. I can always return a shipment and cancel at any time. Even if I never buy another book from Harlequin, the two free books and gifts are mine to keep forever.

114 HDN EEV7   314 HDN EEWK

Name	(PLEASE PRINT)	
Address		Apt.
City	State/Prov.	Zip/Postal Code

Signature (if under 18, a parent or guardian must sign)

Mail to Harlequin Reader Service®:

IN U.S.A.	IN CANADA
P.O. Box 1867	P.O. Box 609
Buffalo, NY	Fort Erie, Ontario
14240-1867	L2A 5X3

Not valid to current Harlequin Romance subscribers.

Want to try two free books from another line?
Call 1-800-873-8635 or visit www.morefreebooks.com.

* Terms and prices subject to change without notice. NY residents add applicable sales tax. Canadian residents will be charged applicable provincial taxes and GST. This offer is limited to one order per household. All orders subject to approval. Credit or debit balances in a customer's account(s) may be offset by any other outstanding balance owed by or to the customer. Please allow 4 to 6 weeks for delivery.

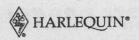
Coming Next Month

#3931 RANCHER AND PROTECTOR Judy Christenberry
Western Weddings
Rancher Jason Barton is all business and steely glares! Rosie Wilson has recently had a run of bad luck—but she's a fighter, and she means business, too. When they get stranded under the starlit Western sky, there's only one place Rosie wants to be: in the arms of the cowboy who has vowed to protect her.

#3932 THE VALENTINE BRIDE Liz Fielding
The Brides of Bella Lucia
Louise Valentine has been offered a job, and Max Valentine wants to help her save the family business. But since discovering she is adopted, Louise is not feeling charitable toward the Valentines. Sparks fly and soon they are both falling hard—will the past stand in the way of a special Valentine wedding?

#3933 ONE SUMMER IN ITALY... Lucy Gordon
It was supposed to be just a holiday… But then, enchanted by the pleading eyes of a motherless little girl and her brooding, enigmatic father, Matteo, Holly is swept away to their luxurious villa. Soon Holly discovers Matteo is hiding some dark secrets—her one summer in Italy is only the beginning....

#3934 THE BOSS'S PREGNANCY PROPOSAL Raye Morgan
Working for her heart-stoppingly handsome boss shouldn't have been hard for Callie, but then he asks her to have a baby with him! Of course, love wouldn't come into the arrangement—as a busy CEO, Grant wants a family, but he's been hurt before. Could sensible Callie be just what he's looking for?

#3935 CROWNED: AN ORDINARY GIRL Natasha Oakley
Just as Prince Sebastian caught a glimpse of normal life, the untimely death of his father, the King of Andovaria, forced him to leave behind his most precious gift—the love of an ordinary girl. Now, years later, Marianne Chambers is in town. Can Seb fight tradition and claim her as his very own princess?

#3936 OUTBACK BABY MIRACLE Melissa James
Heart to Heart
As untamed as the Outback land he masters, cattleman Jake Connors is a mystery to Laila. Something about him calls to her in a way no other man has. But before he can give her his heart, Jake must stop running from the demons of his past. Might Laila's pregnancy surprise be the miracle they both need?